W9-CRS-200

BILL WANNAN SELECTS

Stories From Old Australia

BILL WANNAN SELECTS

Stories From Old Australia

SUN BOOKS · MELBOURNE

Sun Books Pty Ltd
South Melbourne, Victoria, 3205, Australia

First published by Sun Books 1976

National Library of Australia
cataloguing in publication data

Bill Wannan Selects Stories from Old Australia

Simultaneously published, Melbourne, The Macmillan
Company of Australia Pty. Ltd.
ISBN 0 333 21067 0
ISBN 0 7251 0231 4 (Sun Books)

1. Short stories, Australian.
I. Wannan, William Fielding, 1915-, ed.

A823.01

Set in Intertype Plantin by The Type Shop, Burnley, Victoria
Printed in Hong Kong

Contents

Editor's Note

Here, for young readers of all ages, from nine to ninety, are twenty-eight Australian 'tales of common acceptance'—that is, traditional stories based on historical events, several legends, a genuine folktale or two ('The Phantom Bullocky' and 'There's Only Two of Us Here', for example), and some old bush jests.

Although the primary purpose of the collection is to entertain, it will also serve, I hope, to show how certain writers, well known and unknown, have attempted to give literary form, and therefore permanence, to some of the themes of nineteenth century Australian folklore: the noble savage, ghostly happenings, the child lost in the bush, the swearing of teamsters, the exploits of work champions like Crooked Mick of the Speewah, and so on.

The narratives have been arranged in chronological order, according to the year of first appearance in print; however, it has not been possible in all cases to pinpoint the birth date with accuracy.

I am grateful for permissions granted to me to include a number of copyrighted items: to Angus & Robertson for A. B. Paterson's ' The Gundaroo Bullock' from *The Collected Verse of A. B. Paterson*; and to Gordon Williams for 'Haunted Hills' and 'A White Bull Came Mourning'. I must also express my indebtedness to an old friend, John White, for the use of several original texts from his excellent library of Australiana. And finally, my warm thanks go to the Literature Board of the Australia Council whose financial assistance gave me the time to research this and other projects yet to be published.

Bill Wannan

W. KERR (?)

Fisher's Ghost
A Legend of Campbelltown

Of Australia's traditional tales none has attained a wider celebrity than that of the murder of a ticket-of-leave man, Frederick George Fisher, near Campbelltown (NSW) in the year 1826. The crime itself was not very remarkable; and no account of the murder or of the bringing of the perpetrator, George Worral, to justice would, in the ordinary course of events, have sustained the interest of readers over the past century and a quarter. But an extraordinary thing happened. Fisher's vengeful ghost appeared one night to a home-going settler, John Farley. Local suspicion was aroused as to the fate of Fisher who, until then, was generally believed to be paying a visit to England. Fisher's remains were discovered; and the murderer was caught, tried and hanged — thanks to an apparition.

The story has been told and retold countless times. It has been the subject of poems, ballads, sketches, essays and an opera. The first literary expression of the tale follows. It appeared in the March 1836 issue of Tegg's Monthly Magazine. *It was reprinted in Geoffrey C. Ingleton's* True Patriots All *(1952) with a footnote suggesting that the author may well have been W. Kerr, a journalist and editor who founded the Melbourne* Argus. *This version of the tale gives the name of the settler who first saw the ghost as Hurley, not Farley. The reader may be interested to compare the 'Kerr' narrative with that by John Lang, also included in this anthology.*

Suggested further reading: Douglas Stewart, Fisher's Ghost *(1960); Frank Cusack,* True Australian Ghost Stories *(1967).*

Reader, have you ever paid a visit to the town, or rather to the village of Campbelltown? If you have, then you must have observed as you strolled through the village, a large unfinished brick building, fast mouldering to decay, which seems to have been intended at the time of erection for a store. It is now rapidly falling into decay, and the freshness of the grass which covers the sward around it, shows that whatever the cause may be the ruins are not much frequented by the inhabitants of the surrounding cottages. The unfinished building and the land which surrounds it were the property some years ago of a man named Frederick Fisher, who occupied an adjoining cottage, of which scarcely a trace now remains.

Fisher had been originally a prisoner, he had served his time in the employ of a gentleman in the neighbourhood, and had removed to the town, when he obtained his ticket-of-leave. Some years previous to the commencement of our tale, he had received his certificate of freedom, having undergone the sentence which had been awarded him by the laws of his country. He had also soon after he became free obtained a grant of a town allotment and had commenced the building referred to, intending on its completion to occupy one portion of it as a dwelling-house, and to convert the remaining part into a store.

Fisher was but a boy at the time of the commission of the offence which had led to his transportation. His relatives, enraged at the disgrace he had subjected them to by his misconduct, had taken little notice of him after that period; and as he could put no trust in those whom he saw around him, placed in circumstances similar to his own, he had consequently formed no friendship, which might have enabled him to pass his vacant time; his education also, had been much neglected in his youth by those very relatives who were so liberal of their censure after he had gone astray; it is not therefore, a matter of surprise, that his time should have, occasionally, hung heavy on his hands.

His own fireside presented few attractions to him; his conduct, since his arrival in the colony, not having been such as to afford him much gratification in the retrospect; the resolution of amendment he had made whilst in jail and on the passage out, had melted like snow when exposed to the demoralizing influence of the example set by those around him. Fisher, like most of his class, flew for refuge from unpleasant recollections, to the society which the neighbouring tap-room afforded, and sought for that which he found not at home, in quaffing the flowing bowl.

The necessary consequences of conduct such as this soon became apparent, his business, to which, on gaining his freedom, he had paid strict attention, was now neglected, but instead of

endeavouring, by exertion, to extricate himself from the diffi-
culties which began to surround him, he plunged yet deeper into
a life of dissipation, frequenting the purlieus of the tap both day
and night. His inevitable ruin became soon so apparent that his
creditors resolved no longer to brook delay; he was accordingly
arrested and lodged in jail, at the instance of one of their number,
for a debt of £150.

Although Fisher had been weak enough to allow the bad
example of others to lead him astray, he was yet far from having
reached the pitch of depravity which many of his associates had
attained: although he had neglected his business, and spent in
dissipation those means which ought to have been applied to the
liquidation of his debts, he had yet sufficient moral principle remaining, to shudder when one of his drunken associates, named
Worral, suggested the expediency of entering into a scheme to
defraud his creditors by making over to him the whole of his
property which yet remained; making at the same time a private
engagement that it should be restored to him as soon as he was
permitted to leave jail.

The persuasions of Worral, who represented to him the ease
and safety with which he might thus revenge himself on his
creditors and regain possession of his property, without any
incumbrance, soon overcame the feelings of repugnance which
he had first felt, and he consented to make the transfer of all he
possessed to Worral, under these conditions. Mr. P. at whose instance Fisher had been incarcerated, finding that he was not the
owner of the property he had supposed, consented, after some
time, to his liberation, as the only means by which he was likely
ever to recover the amount of his claim. Fisher, immediately on
his release, returned to Campbelltown, exulting in the success
of his scheme.

About a week after Fisher's return, he left his house one evening with the intention, it was supposed, of resorting, according
to his usual custom, to some of the neighbouring ginshops.
Morning came, but his continued absence excited no surprise,
as it was supposed that he had got so drunk the previous night,
as to be unable to return home. As the day wore on, and no signs
of his appearance, a neighbour went to inquire at the various
public-houses whether he had been there. He had not been at
any of his usual haunts, nor had any person seen him since the

previous evening. Many conjectures were made as to the cause of his protracted absence, but no feasible reason could be adduced until the afternoon, when Worral returned from Sydney, whither he said he had on the previous evening, accompanied Fisher, who had sailed early that morning for England in order to avoid the importunities of his creditors, who had lately been rather troublesome to him, some of them having even threatened to lodge him again in jail. This was corroborated by the fact that a vessel did sail for England on that day.

Worral's statement set completely at rest all the conjectures which had previously been afloat as to the cause of Fisher's disappearance, and he was allowed to take undisputed possession of the property on producing Fisher's conveyance. Time wore on, and Fisher's name was almost forgotten or never alluded to, except by the deluded creditors.

About six weeks after Fisher's disappearance, Mr Hurley, a respectable settler in the vicinity of Campbelltown, was returning thence to his residence; he had long been acquainted with Fisher, and it is by no means improbable that his mind reverted to his sudden disappearance when passing the place where he had so long resided; be that as it may, however, no doubt as to Worral's statement ever entered his mind. It was about ten o'clock at night when he left Campbelltown; the moon had risen, but her brilliance was obscured by clouds.

After he had passed the late residence of Fisher, about from five to eight hundred yards, he observed the figure of a man sitting on top of the fence on the same side of the road as the house. On approaching nearer, what was his surprise to recognize distinctly the features of Fisher, whom he had supposed then far on his way to England. He approached the figure with the intention of assuring himself that he had not been deceived by a fancied resemblance. The ghastly appearance which the features presented to his view on his nearer approach struck such a chill of terror in his heart as chained him motionless to the spot. The figure, as he gazed, rose from the fence, and waving its arms pointed in the direction of a small dry creek, which crossed the paddock at that place, and disappeared gradually from his view, apparently following the windings of the creek. The terror which overpowered the faculties of Hurley at this sight defies all powers of description; in a state of stupefaction he left the spot, and endeavoured to obtain an entrance into the nearest house.

How he managed to find his way to the house he has no recollection, but just as he approached it his senses totally forsook him. The noise caused by his head striking the door as he fell alarmed the inmates, who on opening it found him lying in a death-like swoon; he was carried into the house, where he lay for a week in the delirium of a brain fever. The frequent mention of the name Fisher in his ravings, attracted the attention of those who attended him, and conjecture was soon busy at work to ascertain what had driven him into such a state; his known character for sobriety, as well as the testimony of those who had parted from him only a few minutes before, forbade the supposition that it had been caused by drunkenness; and rumour, with her thousand tongues, turned the villagers' heads with vain conjectures as to its probable cause. On the morning of the ninth day of Hurley's illness, he awoke after a long and refreshing sleep in the full possession of his senses, and expressed a wish to those around him that the Police Magistrate should be sent for.

William Howe, Esq., of Glenlee, who then filled the situation of Superintendent of Police for Campbelltown and the surrounding districts, was sent for, and came immediately on being made aware of the circumstances. To him Hurley disclosed what he had seen, and the suspicion of Fisher's having met with foul play, which that sight had impressed on his mind. As soon as Hurley was able to leave his bed, Mr Howe, accompanied by a few constables, among whom was a native black named Gilbert, went, conducted by Hurley, to a place where the apparition had been seen. On closely examining the panel of fencing pointed out, Mr Howe discovered spots of blood. An active search was commenced to discover further traces of the supposed murder, but nothing more was observed.

It was thought advisable to trace the course of the creek in the direction to which the apparition had pointed, and in which it had disappeared. Some small ponds of water still remained in the creek, and these Black Gilbert was directed to explore with his spear; he carefully examined each as he approached it, but the shake of his head denoted his want of success. On approaching a larger pond than any of those he had before searched, the standers-by observed his eyes sparkle, as he exclaimed in a tone of triumph, while yet at some distance from the pool, 'white man's fat sit down here'; as soon as he reached the bank of the pond he thrust his spear into the water, and after some search, he pointed to a particular spot in the water, saying 'white man there'.

The constables were immediately set to work to clear away the water, which was soon effected—and on digging among the sand the remains of a human being in an advanced stage of decomposition were discovered. It became now obvious to all that Fisher (if the remains which had been found were really his) had met with an untimely end. Suspicion alighted on Worral, who was the only person who had reaped any benefit from Fisher's death; and it was remembered also that it was he who had first propagated the story of Fisher's return to England.

Mr Howe caused Worral to be arrested, and the suspicion being confirmed by a body of circumstantial evidence, he was committed to take his trial before the Supreme Court for the murder. The conviction that retributive justice was now about to overtake him had such an effect on his mind that he confessed his guilt. His reason for so barbarous a proceeding arose from the transaction mentioned in the former part of the narrative. Fisher, overjoyed at the success of the scheme by which he had defrauded his creditors, forgot to regain possession of the deed of conveyance by which he had made over his property to Worral. The thought occurred to Worral that, if he could only get Fisher quietly out of the way, he would be able to claim possession of the property in right of that conveyance.

Under the mask of friendship, he was Fisher's companion during the day—and night after night he watched Fisher's motion from the time of his return from jail until the one on which the murder was committed. On that night he was as usual prowling about Fisher's cottage, looking out for an opportunity to attain his ends, when Fisher, tempted by the beauty of the evening, left his house to take a walk, followed at some distance by Worral. At the place where the blood was afterwards discovered, Fisher stopped and leant against the fence, apparently wrapped in deep thought. The assassin had now before him the opportunity he had so long waited for, and taking up a broken panel of fence, he stole quietly behind him, and with one blow of his weapon stretched him lifeless on the ground; he carried the dead body from the scene of the murder to the place where it was afterwards discovered, and buried it deep in the sand. A few weeks after he had made the confession he expiated his crime on the scaffold, imploring with his last breath the forgiveness of his Maker.

CHARLES ROWCROFT

Musquito and the Gipsy's Daughter

Charles Rowcroft, an English visitor to Australia, settled briefly on a Tasmanian pastoral property between 1821 and 1824. He wrote of his experience in Tales of the Colonies, or The Adventures of an Emigrant, *first published in London in 1843. An edition, with much factual material removed and a continuous fictional narrative retained, was published in Hobart in 1916 with the title* The Perils and Adventures of Mr William Thornley, One of the Pioneer Settlers of Van Diemen's Land, 1817-1820.

The interesting aspect of the extract which follows is the depiction of the historical character, the Aboriginal leader Musquito, as a great chieftain and a noble savage. Musquito, born and bred in New South Wales, first experienced white man's justice when he was sent to Norfolk Island for the murder of a lubra. From that 'ocean hell' he was transported to Van Diemen's Land in 1813. He was employed by the authorities at Hobart Town to search out runaway convicts and to track down such formidable outlaws as Mike Howe. In time Musquito became something of a rebel himself. Known throughout the island as the 'Black Outlaw', he led a band of Aborigines, at first peaceably enough but later violently, in raids on settlers' properties in which several colonists were killed.

Captured late in the year 1824, Musquito was placed on trial along with another offender, 'Black Jack'. Henry Melville, in The History of Van Diemen's Land *(1835), gives an ironical view of the legal proceedings:*

> *On the one side was the learned Attorney General, pressing, as in duty bound, the conviction of the offenders against laws brought by the invaders to the country; and on the bench sat a Judge to administer impartially these laws, which neither Musquito nor Black Jack comprehended. 'Convict' witnesses were brought forward, whose evidence was taken and believed, because it was sworn to; and yet these poor, perhaps guilty creatures of the crime imputed to them (which in them was no crime, but retaliation), were called upon for their*

defence!—what mockery! The wretched prisoners were not aware of one tittle of evidence adduced against them, were totally ignorant of having committed crime, and knew not why or wherefore they were placed at the criminal's dock in the Court House, and so many eyes fixed upon them. Both these Aborigines underwent the ordeal of trial twice on one day, and without counsel . . .

Both prisoners, being convicted of wilful murder, were hanged in company with six bushrangers in February 1825.

Suggested further reading: Musquito loomed large in the minds of his contemporaries, white and black, in Van Diemen's Land; and much has been written about him. For a succinct modern account of his career, see Robert Travers, Rogues' March *(1973).*

We drew up on the margin of the tracks of the natives, which were in the direction of the ford; and it seemed as if there had been about twenty of them, to judge from the confused prints of their naked feet.

'I'll bet a guinea,' said Sanders, 'this is what made 'em hide for a while among those mimosas. They saw the natives between them and the ford, and they feared to face them.'

'Keep on,' said the magistrate, 'their tracks lead to the ford—and I think I see some object on the bank of the river.'

He was right; a few minutes' trot brought us to the ford, and by the side of the stream was lying a man in a fustian dress, whose countenance I thought I remembered. On examining him more closely the police recognized a convict.

The poor wretch was still alive, but his skull was pounded in by the waddies of the natives, and his body was pierced in many places by their thin and pointed spears.

'If we could only get him to speak now,' said the constable, 'he might give us some useful information. Scroggs, where's your bottle?'

Upon this the provident Scroggs produced a pint bottle of rum—a sovereign remedy, in his opinion, for all disorders.

'What's the use of giving him rum if he's dead?' remonstrated Scroggs; 'it's only wasting it that way.'

'He's not dead,' said Sanders, 'though it won't be long first, seemingly. Let us try to make him speak; he may be able to tell us of the other one. It's Bill Simmons, one of the biggest rascals in the whole colony, but that's no matter now. Give us the bottle.'

He raised up the expiring wretch, and Sanders poured down his throat a portion of the rum, while the magistrate dashed some cold water from the river over his head and face. For a considerable time the man gave no other signs of life than a faint breathing, and it was not until after the lapse of two hours, which seemed to us two ages, that he was able to articulate.

'They have got the child,' murmured out the dying man.

'Who have got the child?'

'The natives——they——attacked——me in——the ford.'

'And your companion, where is he?'

'I saw him swimming in the river——but——in his haste——he abandoned the child——to save himself——and the natives took the child——the Gipsy——the Gipsy——the Gipsy's child!'

'Did the natives kill the child?' asked I, full of anxious horror at the probable fate of the poor girl.

'They——have——killed me. Their waddies——my head—— spears——child——carried off——'

'How long is it,' asked the magistrate, 'since they attacked you?'

'I——don't know——it——was——just——at——daybreak. I didn't——like to pass the bridge——so——I made for the ford—— and the natives——attacked us——and they have taken the—— child——.'

'What's o'clock?' asked Sanders.

'Half-past ten,' said I.

'Then the natives have got the start of us by about four hours and a half,' resumed the constable; 'and if they have taken to the hills it will be a difficult job to follow them on horseback.'

'We can easily track them in the snow,' observed the magistrate.

'While the snow lasts,' replied the constable; 'but, by the look of Ben Lomond, we shall have a change of weather, and there's a northerly wind this morning, and that, with the sun, will soon melt this snow. Following the natives in the bush is no easy matter. A white man might as well try to track a bird as a native in the bush!'

'I shall go after them,' said the magistrate; 'what do you say, Thornley; shall we leave this little girl to the mercy of the savages?'

'I'm ready to go with you,' said I, 'but let us go prepared; this is a bad time of the year for bushing it. Is there no place near here, Sanders, where we could borrow some kangaroo rugs, and get a supply of provisions?'

'I have it!' said Sanders; 'Mark's sheep-run is not more than two miles from the ford, and if he will let one of his shepherds, Black Tom, go with us—he's a Sydney native—we'll set a black fellow to hunt black fellows, and come over them that way.'

'Come on, then,' said the magistrate, 'and lose no time. I will go with you to remove any objection. Stay! the dying man is going to speak again. I think he understood what we were saying. What is it, my man?' he added, in a soothing tone to the dying man; 'what have you got to say?'

'Mus––quee––to!' said the man, with his last breath.

'Musquito!' said Sanders, 'then there's no time to be lost; that's the cruellest savage that ever tormented a colony; he kills for killing sake, without reason.'

'I have had a taste of him,' said the magistrate. 'There's no time to be lost, if we are to save the child.'

The magistrate, guided by Sanders, immediately galloped off; and in less time than we expected, they returned at a brisk pace, laden with kangaroo rugs, and various necessaries for a bush expedition, and followed by Tom, a fine tall native of the continental island of Australia, dressed with much neatness, in a cloth jacket and trousers of good texture; the civilized natives soon catching the colonial predilection for cloth of a superior quality.

'Will not the native, being on foot, retard us?' inquired I. 'He can never keep up with our horses.'

'Never fear,' said Sanders; 'if our horses can keep up with him we shall do very well. Now, Tom, my boy, are you ready?'

Tom nodded his head.

'Which way are you going to take us!' Tom looked at the tracks, among which the prints of tiny feet were plainly discernible, and pointed to the hills.

'Now,' said the magistrate, 'for another adventure. I never had a hunt after natives before. Not the best of weather for lying out at nights; but it would never do to leave that little girl to be butchered by Musquito!'

We moved on at a good pace, Tom with his long legs keeping our horses just beyond a quick walk, and we were soon buried in the deep recesses of the woods. The dense mass of spreading branches, with their winter leaves of sombre green, which formed a canopy high above our heads, had allowed but little snow to fall on the forest ground; but there were ample signs of the natives to enable the sagacious Sydney black to guide us through the intricacies of the tall straight stems of the stringy-bark trees, with their ragged, shreddy coats, without hesitation. Ever and anon he would turn round to us, without discontinuing his course, and displaying, with a self-satisfied grin, his formidable rows of ivory teeth, he would point to the track, and seek, with his piercing and restless black eyes, deep set in his woolly head, for our approbation of his sagacity.

It occupied us nearly two hours to pass through the forest, and we then emerged into an ample plain nearly clear of the trees, resembling a vast park. The noonday sun had melted nearly all the snow, and it was only here and there, under the shade of some gigantic gum-tree or umbrageous mimosa, that any signs of it were visible. We were glad to get rid of the snow, as, under the guidance of the black, we had no fear of losing the tracks of the natives, and we pushed on without stopping for nearly twenty miles, in a south-easterly direction, over a fine country of undulating hill and plain, till we came to the foot of a tier of low hills, on which were scattered a few trees of the she-oak. These trees present a scraggy appearance to the eye, but their wood is much prized as fuel, from its pleasing fragrance and good qualities for burning. It is not easy to get a plank from these trees of more than six or eight inches in width, but, when polished, it is admirably adapted for ornamental furniture. Here we made a pause to rest our horses, which we tethered out by the hide ropes, which we carried with us on the front of our saddles, giving them the range of a circle of about eighty feet in diameter to feed on the native grass, shifting them occasionally as their food grew scanty. The constables kindled a fire and proceeded with the usual arrangements for a bush meal.

They put a handful of black tea into the kettle, which Scroggs bore in his portion of the luggage, and set it on to boil—tea forming the favourite beverage of settlers of every degree in their bush expeditions. The dexterous black, who carried a long-shanked, narrow axe, quickly sliced from an adjacent gum-tree some pieces of bark, which formed extempore plates and dishes, and some steaks of young beef being duly boiled, aided by one of the dampers, which formed part of our provisions, we made, with the relish of hunger, a satisfactory repast. The constables then got up a second edition of the feast with some additional supplies, for Black Tom, not liking to remain idle during our banquet, had contrived to catch three kangaroo-rats and a bandicoot, which he disembowelled with much delicacy, and threw them in their furry coats on some close embers of the fire. Scroggs produced from the recesses of a mysterious garment a bottle of rum, but it was unanimously decided that this luxury should be reserved as a medicine for special occasions. Much to the disappointment of that thirsty individual, therefore, the cork remained undrawn, and the disconsolate Scroggs was obliged to solace himself with a pannikin of hot tea from the boiling kettle. Our rough repast ended, we proceeded on our way till the sinking of the sun behind the snow-topped mountains to the west warned us to turn our attention to the means of passing the night; for the nights in the winter season in Van Diemen's Land are too cold to allow of their being passed with impunity in the open air. As we felt the fullest confidence of coming up with the natives, we did not push our horses to the extreme, for we knew that Musquito and his mob would not travel many days without making a stop in some locality favourable for the collection of gum and the resort of opossums. We had but one axe among us, but there were more than one who knew well how to use it, the cleverest of whom was the Sydney black; so that in a short time they managed to erect two bush-huts well covered in with heavy branches. The opening of the huts being next to the fire, which was kept up all night, we contrived, with the aid of our warm kangaroo rugs, to pass the night without inconvenience.

Towards the early morning the air became frosty, and the next day, under a clear sky and a brilliant sun, we continued our pursuit of the natives. At noon the air became mild and warm, and if it had not been for our apprehensions of the calamitous fate of the child to whose rescue we were hastening, we should have enjoyed the beautiful scenery of the almost unexplored country through which we travelled; but a second day and night having passed without coming up with the natives, our uneasiness increased to a pitch of painful anxiety. We could discover no trace of the little foot, nor indeed could our less acute sense of sight detect any marks of the retiring natives, although to the black's stronger and more sensitive organs the marks were so plain as to cause him no apparent trouble to pursue. We consoled ourselves, however, with the reflection that the absence of any mark of the child's foot which Tom could not trace might be accounted for by her having been carried in the arms of the natives, though what could be their object, or the object of Musquito in bearing her away, we were at a loss to conjecture, and feared the worst.

With these doubts and fears we passed an uneasy night, the more so as our provisions being nearly exhausted, we could not keep up the animal strength to counteract the depression of the spirits. Under circumstances so favourable for the opening of the grog bottle, the longing Scroggs made several insinuating attempts to get our assent to that measure but it was steadily resisted, and with a stoicism on the part of his reflected coadjutor which I particularly admired.

'Cold work this,' said Scroggs to Sanders; 'and cold water is poor stuff to put heart into a man. A fire is very well to warm the outside, but the inside is the place to keep up the heat; then it spreads all over one in a glow! It's surprising how small a quantity of spirit—a single glass or so, I've often tried it—will warm a man's whole body, to the very tips of one's fingers!'

'To the tip of your nose, you ought to say, old buck,' rejoined his mate, 'for you have put that sponge of yours into such a glow some time, that it has never got cool again.'

'None of your nonsense; it's all owing to smoking out of a short pipe; I went to sleep with it one night in my mouth, and I slept so sound, though I had drunk nothing to speak of, that the end of my nose got briled on the bowl of the pipe before I woke up.'

'I wish you had thought to bring two bottles, instead of one,' said Sanders, 'then you might have soaked your nose in one and kept the other. But you don't know what may happen in the bush, and a sup of rum may save a man's life. Better keep it till it's wanted.'

'But it is wanted,' persisted the persevering Scroggs; 'I declare I feel so queer I don't know what to make of it; and that bit of opossum that I was fool enough to eat makes me smell all turpentine. What harm could it do,' he added, in a melancholy tone, 'if I took only the least sip in the world—just a taste—only a smell at the bottle?'

But Sanders was firm, and as Scroggs stood too much in awe of the magistrate to venture on so flagrant a breach of duty as a burglary on the rum bottle, he betook himself sadly to bed and covering himself up with his kangaroo rug, after a few dolorous moanings, the sounds which proceeded from his fiery nose proclaimed that he was sound asleep.

The next morning found them much less fresh than the preceding one, and no one seemed inclined for conversation, our spirits being damped by the unsuccessful pursuit, and by the contemplation of the uncertain distance to which we might be led in our chase and of the uncertain time which might be consumed in it. We had bivouacked at the base of a tier of hills, and it was not without anxiety that we shared the remainder of our provisions and prepared for the steep ascent before us.

We had not proceeded far, however, when, on some moist ground beneath a spring, which trickled down the hill, Black Tom pointed out to us the fresh mark of a native foot. We were heading our horses up the ascent, and it was with lively curiosity that we regarded the sign of the probable propinquity of the natives. We immediately looked to our arms, wiped our flints, renewed our primings, and examined our barrels, to see that the charges had not become loosened in the journey. The prospect of danger spread animation among the party, mixed with some anxiety, for we had by this time penetrated into a part of the country never, perhaps, trodden before by a white man's foot, and far removed from all assistance. We advanced, therefore, with great precaution till we got close to the summit of the hill, when the magistrate directed us to stand still, and motioned the black to reconnoitre.

Tom advanced cautiously and silently upwards, crawling on his belly, and winding his way like a snake over the tufts of grass, till he was enabled to project his black poll—hardly to be distinguished from the rough logs of charred timber that lay about over the ridge of the hill. For some seconds he remained motion-less, and then, withdrawing himself by imperceptible degrees from his place of observation, he communicated to us the result of his discovery.

'Black fellows in bottom,' said Tom softly; 'Musquito with 'em.'

'What are they doing?' asked the constable.

'Make fire——and eat.'

'Is the piccaninny with them?' said I.

'Can't see. Go behind trees, there,' continued Tom, pointing to the right, 'then you see all.'

On the right was a clump of bushes, to which we bent our steps. Leaving our horses under the charge of the constables, we edged around the declivity of the hill and crept up to the top, where we stationed ourselves behind the bushes. From this pos-ition we observed the natives in the hollow below. They had evi-dently arrived at a spot at which they proposed to sojourn for a while, for they had raised up in two or three places, and with more than usual care, break-winds formed of branches and trees, and lined with wide strips of bark. These rude protections from the wind were about four feet high, and we remarked that one apart from the rest had the distinction of an attempt at a roof, but of dimensions not more than sufficient to contain a single person. Large fires were lighted before the break-winds, at which some of the natives reclined; others were standing listlessly here and there, and some of the women were engaged in tending their children. Almost the whole party was naked; but one man, whom by his stature and bearing we recognized as Musquito, was distinguished by a black hat, with waistcoat and trousers, and one or two of the women had something which looked like old and dirty blankets thrown over their shoulders. We remained for some time watching them from our hiding-place, but we could observe no signs of the child whom we had come so far to rescue; and we had had misgivings of her safety. Having made all the observations in our power, we retreated back to the brow of the hill, and consulted together as to the best course to pursue.

'If you would be pleased to take my advice, sir,' said Sanders, 'I would wait till night, when the natives are afraid to move about, and then, by advancing two together, we might take them by surprise, and the first thing would be to shoot down Musquito, and the men of the party, and then if they run away with the child—that is, if they haven't murdered it already, which I think most likely—we can pursue them with our horses, for they're terribly afraid of a horse; they think it bites, and fights with its fore-legs.'

'I confess,' said the magistrate, 'I am very much disappointed not to see the little girl; our object is to release her, not to slaughter these naked savages. Did you ever know them to eat a white person? Let us find out from Tom; do you speak to him, Sanders; he knows you, and would tell you perhaps more freely than us.'

'Tom,' said Sanders, 'black fellow eat white piccaninny?'

Tom looked suspiciously at the constable with his deep-set, restless eyes, one of the characteristics of the natives of Australia, and seemed unwilling to reply; for the Sydney blacks, as well as the few who have communication with the settlements of Van Diemen's Land, are well aware of the horror of the whites at the practice of eating human flesh.

'Tom never eat man,' said Sanders, coaxingly, 'no—never; but bad black fellow eat man, and eat piccaninny sometimes?'

'Bad black fellow eat man sometimes,' replied Tom, 'while he very angry and fight; me never eat man.'

'No, not you; but black man eat white man, sometimes?'

'Yees.'

'And eat white piccaninny sometimes; bad black fellow.'

'Yees——bad black fellow.'

'The nasty inhuman savages!' exclaimed Scroggs, who was within hearing, holding the horses. 'To think of that poor little girl being eat by those black devils, just as if she was mutton or beef! Here, Sanders, come and put your hand in my pocket, and take out the bottle of rum; take it, I say! I, for one, will give it up, and let the natives have it for the child. I should like to have just one sup of it before it goes; but never mind, I'll give it all, rather than the child should be eat up by those black rascals!'

'Well done, Scroggs,' said the magistrate; 'depend upon it this generous instance of self-denial shall not be forgotten, for I know the effort which it must have cost you; but I think we can manage without putting your virtue to so severe a trial. Tom,' said he to our guide, 'will you go and try if you can see a little white piccaninny among the black fellows? Piccaninny so high,' describing the height of a child of six or seven years of age.

Tom understood what was said to him in English much more easily than he could find words to reply. He comprehended the magistrate in a moment, and looked on the ground for a while in a thoughtful attitude.

'Me go,' said he.

Without further talk, for the natives are remarkably taciturn and sententious among themselves, as well as among the whites, Tom proceeded to strip himself of the encumbrance of his clothes, even to his shoes and stockings, and displayed himself in the natural undisguise of our great progenitor, Adam. The disencumbered Tom formed his plan on the instant, and taking a wide circuit to the left, he was soon lost to view, leaving us in a state of anxious and nervous expectation.

After the lapse of an hour he returned, and in the cold apathetic manner of the natives he communicated his information with his usual sententious brevity—.

'White piccaninny with black fellows.'

'That's capital!' said the magistrate; 'the poor little thing is alive, at any rate. How does she look, Tom?'

But Tom did not understand this question but, seeing that an answer was expected, he replied—.

'Piccaninny in little house,' describing by gesture the single break-wind which we had observed from behind the bushes.

'What are they going to do with the piccaninny?' said I.

'Eat her, I'll be bound,' said Scroggs; 'that's what they're going to do with her; and they are fattening her up in that pen as we do a lamb, till she's in good condition. The black villains! Let us march right at 'em and shoot 'em down, every one. I'm ready for it!'

'There is something in this,' observed the magistrate, 'which I cannot understand. It is difficult sometimes to penetrate into the motives of savages; but as they seem at present to be in a peaceful humour, I think our best plan is to send on Tom a little in advance to parley with them, and to assure them that we have no hostile intentions. We can follow immediately behind him on horseback, with our arms ready, in case of their showing fight; but as we shall take them by surprise, I think it very likely that they will not attempt any resistance. You all know that it is the particular desire of the Colonial Government, which is conformable, indeed, with sound policy and with humanity, never to commit an aggression on the natives uselessly and without the most pressing necessity; but on all occasions to treat them with benevolence and tenderness, and to endeavour to win them over by acts of kindness, instead of alienating them by the wanton or thoughtless exercise of superior power.'

'If you please, sir,' said Sanders, 'Musquito has committed more than one murder, and he's a Sydney black and ought to know better. We have orders from Camp to endeavour to take him if we should have the opportunity.'

'We shall act according to circumstances,' replied the magistrate. 'At present our object is to rescue the child from the clutches of the savages; and in doing that we must endeavour to avoid shedding blood.'

I agreed with the magistrate in the propriety of his mode of action, and although I had a strong presentiment that there would be a murderous conflict, I relied on the superiority of our arms and our horses, and had little doubt of the result.

We descended the hill, therefore, and forming ourselves into the order laid down by our leader, we moved round the hill to the right, that we might reach the level ground before we could be perceived by the natives, and advancing at a moderate pace, we soon found ourselves in front of their curious habitations.

The Sydney black preceded us about twenty yards in advance and, as soon as he arrived within easy speaking distance of the natives, we pulled up, and with much anxiety waited for the issue of his conference. He had previously resumed his clothes, but it was easy for the natives to perceive by his colour and his features that he was allied to their general race. To our extreme surprise—although the aborigines of Van Diemen's Land have a strong antipathy to the natives of the continental island—our messenger was allowed to approach their fires without exciting the slightest visible sensation. Their simulated unconcern might have been produced, perhaps, by the sight of our party on horseback; but the strangeness of this unexpected apathy on the part of Musquito and his companions made us fear some treachery, and we looked round to try if we could perceive any appearance of an ambuscade; but we could detect nothing to excite suspicion. I have often had occasion to observe the dull, listless, and almost idiotic appearance of the natives of Van Diemen's Land when not excited by hunger or some passionate desire. It has struck me that, in this respect they much resemble the unthinking beasts of the field, so inanimate and log-like is their usual manner. The women will sometimes chatter a little, for it seems nature makes them all alike as to that matter, but the men have the most reserved and taciturn habit of any race of savages that I have known or read of. The strange contrast of their silence and immobility with the yells and wildness for which we were prepared, filled us with a vague sort of superstitious fear, which was heightened by the chilly stillness of the vast wilderness in which we were now enclosed.

In the meantime a monosyllable 'corrobara' had taken place between our guide and the chief of the sable community, the meaning of which Tom concentrated in the following brief communication—

'Musquito say, you come.'

'Why, what is the meaning of this?' said the magistrate. 'They don't show any signs of fear, nor do they look as if they thought of fighting! Is there some stratagem in this? What do you think of it, Thornley?'

'Upon my word', I replied, 'this takes me so much by surprise, I don't know what to think of it. Sanders, you know their ways, do you see any of their waddies or spears about?'

'One can never tell, sir,' said Sanders, 'what those treacherous savages are at; they're always hatching some devilry or other. You see, sir, I take it we have come on one of their places for encamping, if you can call those bits of break-winds camps. But Musquito can be civil enough, sometimes. Scroggs, you've often come across Musquito, what is he after now?'

'He's always after some wickedness,' responded Scroggs; 'but I think the natives are going to have a feast. Don't you see that string of opossums yonder, by the blue-gum tree? and there's something hanging up inside the bushes; the Lord have mercy on us, it must be the child! and the black devils are going to cook it for their dinner!'

'The child!' exclaimed the magistrate; 'no, impossible! Tom saw the child alive a quarter of an hour ago! Go, Tom, ask

Musquito if he has got the white man's piccaninny.'

Tom made the inquiry accordingly, and presently returned with a reply.

'Musquito say, white man kill piccaninny, Musquito kill white man. Piccaninny in piccaninny house—there.'

'This is very extraordinary,' said the magistrate; 'the most extraordinary thing that has occurred to me in all my adventures in the colony. What can be Musquito's object in this? However, as they seem quietly disposed, let us advance close to them, and try to get possession of the poor child by peaceable means.'

'Better let two of us stand on guard, in case of any attack,' suggested the constable; 'no need sir, for us all to be sacrificed.'

'That is a very prudent precaution, Sanders; do you and Scroggs remain here in charge of the horses, and I and Mr Thornley will go to them on foot—that is, if Mr Thornley has no objection.'

'None in the least,' said I; 'the best way with savages, and all animals in general, is to show that you have no fear of them.'

'Better take my bottle of rum,' suggested Scroggs, in the exuberance of his generosity; 'let Musquito have a sup at it, and perhaps that will put him in good humour.'

'No, no,' said the magistrate, 'keep the rum till we want it. A savage is awkward enough to deal with when he is sober, but with a little rum in him he is worse than a madman. Now, Thornley, let us go among them boldly.'

Accordingly, we went up to Musquito, who was standing by one of the fires in front of the little wigwam in which we had been given to understand the little girl of whom we were in search was secreted. He had, I thought, the same stupid and sullen look which I had remarked on other occasions, as he stood in the listless and dozing attitude which was usual with him when not engaged in any hunting or predatory expedition. A close investigation, however, might detect in his half-shut, but ever restless, eyes, a watchfulness that allowed nothing to escape his observation. I confess it was not without a little nervous apprehension, and some slight bumping in the region of my left side, that I approached the formidable savage in his lair. He raised up his eyes and glanced at us, but gave no sign of recognition, or of being affected by our presence.

We remained for a brief space in this unpleasant position, with the awkward feeling of having intruded on a gentleman's privacy without an invitation. Neither of us spoke—my friend being under the same difficulty as myself to hit upon an appropriate topic by which to commence a conversation with this chief of a band of savages, and the usual salutation of a 'very fine day' seeming to me, under the circumstances, inappropriate to the individual and the occasion; but I was relieved by the magistrate breaking silence.

'Much kangaroo, Musquito, in this part of the country?'

'Boomah——there,' replied Musquito, pointing out an immense kangaroo in the bushes, which had attracted the attention of the horrified Scroggs.

My excellent friend presuming, I suppose, that eating and drinking among friends facilitated conversation, and being stimulated besides by certain internal promptings that his fast had continued for more than a reasonable time, immediately intimated to his new acquaintance his inclination for a steak.

Musquito uttered a few words to one of his retinue, and without further ceremony some pieces of the kangaroo were brought to us; we motioned to them to put the venison on the fire, which they did with a readiness to oblige which inspired us with some confidence in their present sincerity.

When the meat was cooked, we sat down on the ground on which Musquito also squatted down opposite. Some of his companions stood at a little distance, eyeing us with much curiosity, but without rudeness; and in this way, with a charming absence of all ceremony, we partook of a social meal with our new acquaintance, but in perfect silence.

Thinking the occasion favourable, I suggested to my friend the expediency of propitiating our host by a glass of rum, as an appropriate introduction to the object of our journey. The magistrate agreed with me, and called quietly to Scroggs to bring the bottle and a pannikin.

I observed that Musquito gave a flash with his eyes at the magistrate's call, and gathered up his legs under him ready for a spring, upon which I instantly called to Scroggs—

'Show the bottle of rum!'

Scroggs raised on high his long-cherished bottle, at the view of which I saw that Musquito's eyes resumed their usual expression, and he quietly returned to his former position of repose. Meanwhile the disappointed Scroggs, with his mouth watering at the sight of a repast in which he did not share, and his eyes becoming tearful at the prospect of the total consumption of his beloved rum, approached with slow and reluctant steps to resign his treasure.

'These savages, sir,' said he, in an insinuating way, to the magistrate, 'are very suspicious——very. If you like, sir, I will taste a little of the rum first—that he may see it is all right, and that we mean no harm to him. Allow me to take out the cork?'

'Make haste back,' said the magistrate, 'and mount your horse, that you may be ready to act in case of need. This rum may be of service to us, and we don't want it for our own drinking; we can get plenty more when we go home.'

So saying, my friend took summary possession of the bottle which the disconsolate Scroggs relinquished with a pitiable sigh, and the salt and savour of life having now departed from him, he resumed his seat lugubriously on the back of his horse with his hapless body, leaving his soul behind him in the bottle.

The magistrate poured into the pannikin a portion of the rum with the same seriousness with which it might be supposed he would have offered a libation to the infernal gods, and, proffering it to the presiding deity of the spot, that condescending personage [tossed] it down with an off-handed dexterity which would have done honour to an inhabitant of the far-famed St Giles in the mother country, and with a gusto which overcame the habitual reserve of a native. He evinced his delectation at the imbibing of the liquor by a grim smile, which made me involuntarily grasp my fowling-piece a little closer, and slapping his breast, he held out the pannikin for a fresh supply. But we thought this a fit opportunity to enter into some sort of treaty for the restoration of the child.

'Musquito kill white man?' said the magistrate: 'why Musquito kill white man?'

'White man great rascal,' replied Musquito; 'try kill piccaninny——Musquito kill him.'

'Why Musquito take piccaninny?' pursued my friend; 'Musquito want to keep piccaninny and make her gin to black man?'

Musquito shook his head, and it seemed to me if he had known how he would have laughed at this inquiry.

'Piccaninny white!' said he; 'not good for black man.'

'Why take piccaninny?' persisted my friend; 'why save her from bad white man?'

It seemed that Musquito suddenly understood what the magistrate was driving at, for his countenance assumed an appearance almost of intelligence, and he immediately replied—

'Gipsy's piccaninny; Gipsy die; Gipsy good to Musquito—— he Musquito's brother; Musquito not let bad white man kill Gipsy's piccaninny.'

My friend and I gazed at each other with astonishment at these words, and, reading each other's thoughts, we could not but admire the strange concatenation of events which had preserved the life of the bushranger's daughter from such imminent perils! But as I had been constituted guardian of that deceased character's child, I considered that there was a means of easy understanding, if I could make the native comprehend the nature of my legal and social position in respect of his temporary ward.

'Gipsy,' said I, 'Musquito's brother.'

'Gipsy, Musquito's brother,' repeated the black chief.

Thought I to myself, the Gipsy's family would not consider themselves very much flattered by this unexpected claim on their relationship by my black friend here, but at any rate he has done one good action to atone for his multitude of crimes, and so I will not flinch from claiming any right to be considered as a member of the family.

'Musquito,' said I, 'you know me?' He had been more than once at my house with his mob, and had been regaled with damper and boiling-hot tea, plentifully sweetened with brown sugar, not forgetting an occasional glass of rum.

'You, Mister Thornley?' said Musquito.

'Yes,' said I, 'and I Gipsy's brother!'

Musquito gave me a quick look, which none but a savage could give, in which was expressed the blended wonder and suspicion which my assumption of relationship with the Gipsy had excited, and I continued—

'Gipsy, Musquito's brother; Gipsy, Thornley's brother; Thornley, Musquito's brother.'

I wished to lead the savage by this ingenious process of ratiocination, as my friend the magistrate called it, in his jocose way, to consider me as an intimate friend and relation, for my object was to get possession of the child, with his concurrence, so as to avoid bloodshed. Musquito mused, I observed, for a while, on these words, and then, with the caution of the savage, he asked—

'Why you Gipsy's brother?'

'The Gipsy,' said I, 'when bad white man kill him, say to me—— "Give bread and meat to my piccaninny——little——so big",' said I, describing the size of a child of six or seven years of age. 'I say to Gipsy, "Thornley, Gipsy's brother." '

Musquito rose from his sitting position when I had said this, and spoke to one of his people, who disappeared, and presently returned with a tall and slender young lady of a bright black colour, who, from her air and pretentions, we immediately concluded was the favourite gin of the grim Musquito. A soldier's old jacket, without buttons and which, with a graceful negligence, remained open in front, formed an airy spencer suitable for summer or for winter wear, and a red cotton handkerchief tied around her woolly black poll gave her a superior air, which distinguished her from her less favoured associates of the seraglio. No other article of dress than that of which we have made modest mention, prevented the free exercise of her supple and well-formed limbs. As an honest historian I am obliged to record that her nose was very broad and flat; but her eyes were large and bright. Various coquettish devices depicted in a mixture of resinous gum and red ochre formed a striking relief to the monotonous hue of her sable skin, and a fish-bone stuck through her nose added a finish to the splendour of her personal appearance.

To this amiable divinity Musquito gave some brief directions, and the lady retiring, quickly re-appeared, leading by the hand the timid and shrinking form of the Gipsy's daughter. I have often thought that when her fancy recalls in after-life the romantic scenes of her early youth, the recollection of this memorable day must form a curious contrast with her present fortunes. She raised up her large black eyes, which instantly reminded me of the last wild look of the Gipsy bushranger, and sought among us for some familiar face; but meeting only with the countenances of strangers, she cast them down again in disappointment and sadness, as if doubtful whether to regard the white strangers as friends or foes.

'Georgiana,' said I, softly.

The little thing started at the secret name, and clasping her tiny hands, she stood with one foot advanced, trembling and irresolute, while she searched me with her lustrous eyes, to discover in me some trace of a former friend.

I think I never saw so beautiful a child; she was the very picture of loveliness, and possessing that indefinable and irresistible charm with which infancy and innocence never fail to move the coldest human heart. Struck with the desolate condition of the child, and possessed with the sacred nature of the trust that I had taken on me, I held out my arms, and said to her in tones which touched her little heart—

'Come to me, my poor little orphan girl; you shall be a daughter among my children, and I will be a friend and a father to you.'

The child screamed with sudden joy, bursting into tears she bounded into my arms, and with passionate sobs hid her little face in my bosom.

The very savages were affected by the scene. The women gathered round us, gazing with earnest interest, and the harsher lineaments of the faces of the men became softened at the touch of nature, which makes the whole world kin.

'Look out, sir,' cried Sanders, who, with Scroggs, had approached in this moment of excitement close to the mingled group; 'take care they don't take you at a disadvantage. You never know when to trust a native.'

'You've dropped the bottle,' whined Scroggs; 'there it is under your legs, and in another moment it will be broken, and all the rum will be lost.'

'And now,' said the magistrate to me, 'let us get back to some place of settlement without loss of time, while we are all in good humour. We can easily carry the child with us on horseback. Now, my men,' he continued to the constables, 'keep your eyes about you; home's the word!'

JOHN SHERER

The Man They Couldn't Kill

From John Sherer, The Gold-Finder of Australia *(1853).*

Similar stories abound in Australian folklore. First of them all is the true tale of Joseph Samuels who, in September 1803, at Sydney, was reprieved after three unsuccessful attempts in one morning had been made to hang him.

'But,' cried [Charlie] raising his voice as he suddenly recollected some story illustrative of the kind of conversation in which they were engaged, 'but did ye ever hear o' Radley's heid—the convict that escaped into the Bush, and had a skull either sae thick or sae hard that a musket-bullet could na get in til't?'

'No,' replied Brown. 'Where did he come from?'

'Just from whaur ye cam frae, or the Irish island next tae ye yonder,' returned Charlie with a smile.

'Are you sure it was not from Scotland, Charlie?'

'Perfectly! We have nae Radleys in Scotland. The family names o' our country are easily known from there a' maistly having been celebrated in border wars or clannish feuds, o' which there's no sae mony noo as there used tae be; Gude be praised!'

'And what about this Radley, then, Charlie?' asked Brown.

'Ou, naething; but only he was an extraordinary sort o' character. His history in this very country is somewhat strange. He was a convict, sent out mony years ago for some o' his ill-gaits at hame; but the atmosphere even o' this country, pure as it is, worked little amendment in him. But I will tell you what he related himsel', when he was apprehended after having escaped into the Bush here, and before he was ta'en out o' this, to gie an account o' himsel' in anither world.' And Charlie narrated the following incidents in the life of this man, which we put into a form more generally comprehensible than the rude Scotticisms with which, either from affectation or some other foible, he occasionally—for he could express himself in perfectly good English when he liked—so plentifully interlarded his discourse.

It would seem that this man had escaped from the degrading bondage to which his own misdeeds had subjected him, and, taking to the Bush, pursued the life of a wandering fugitive, living upon the natural products of the woods, the wild animals which his skill enabled him to catch, and by the depredations which his courage enabled him to commit. A reward had been offered for his apprehension, and a man by whom he had frequently been harboured determined, at last, to betray him into the hands of the Government. With a view to this end, this traitor—for, in my opinion, he merits the name—had two constables concealed in his hut when Radley was expected to seek it as a refuge and a place of security. He came accordingly; but as he was approaching the door with a companion, he had a presentiment that all was not right, and expressed himself to that effect. Indeed, so strongly was this feeling impressed upon him, that he would have turned away, had his companion not reasoned with him upon the improbability of his being betrayed by one who so often had proved his friend by protecting him in his former emergencies. Without being in the smallest degree convinced by the arguments of the other, he advanced upon his destiny, and, when near enough, was fired upon by the constables. He was wounded in the arm, and captured, with his companion. The latter being immediately marched off by the constables to the next magistrate, Radley was left in the charge of his quondam friend.

'Well, Spokes,' said Radley, for that was the name of his betrayer, 'this is not the treatment I expected from you.'

'I know that,' replied the other with a heartless grin, and added, 'If it had, you would scarcely have paid me a visit this time.'

'It is strange,' returned Radley, 'but something told me that you were about to give me up to the Philistines; and had it not been for my chum, I'm d——d if I'd a been here. That I wouldn't!'

'Oh, never mind,' returned the other, who really seems to have had a heart equally bad with himself, and a great deal more cowardly, 'Oh, never mind, you will only be hanged; and as there is neither a God nor a Devil, that is of little consequence.'

The cool kind of chuckle with which this atheistical expression was accompanied produced a far deeper impression upon Radley than did the expression itself; and he changed the conversation, and artfully drew his betrayer into the memory of the confidence and friendship which had always hitherto subsisted between them. By degrees, the heart of Spokes became touched with sympathy. He considered the situation of Radley, and the probability of the brief tenure which he now held of existence, remembered that he had shared some of his former spoils, and, by request, gave him his bed to lie on, and covered him with a kangaroo-rug. This was all that Radley wanted; and, under pretence of suffering great pain from the severity of his wound, he set himself vigorously to extricate his hands from the cord with which they were bound.

The suspicion of Stokes was now completely lulled asleep, and Radley, in his bed, was by this time free from his bonds. Courageous by nature, and artful by experience and habit, he solicited a drop of water to allay the burning thirst with which he said he was tortured from the pain of his wounds. 'You, Spokes,' said he, 'will do me the kindness to put the cup to my lips, seeing that I cannot do it for myself.'

'Oh, yes, Radley,' returned Spokes, 'I'll do that.' And putting down his loaded gun to procure the beverage, Radley sprang from his bed, seized the weapon, and, uttering a laugh of triumph, pointed it at the head of his betrayer. 'Now, you dog,' cried he, 'prepare for death!'

'O Radley!' cried Spokes, who was entirely destitute of the courage of the other, 'for God's sake, spare my life.'

'Doubly d——d and anointed villain!' returned Radley, 'hypocrite three times distilled in the gloomiest pit of perdition, how can you ask me to spare your life for the sake of God, when, but a few minutes ago, you said that, as there is neither God nor devil, I need not mind hanging? I'll see your blood, you blackhearted scoundrel! If it is for nothing else but to know its colour. I will not, however, lest the report of this gun should make an alarm; but if ever I come across you again, your fate is sealed.' On saying this, he left the hut, and once more became a free ranger of the woods.

Wandering about for a considerable time, like a solitary savage, and occasionally drawing near the habitation of some hut-keeper to solicit charity or perpetrate crime, life itself, one would think, would have become intolerable; but, by degrees, he surrounded himself with a band of escaped convicts as desperate as himself, and pursued a species of brigandage as terrifying to the settlers as it was often dangerous to himself. It was whilst he held the command of this gang that he fell in with this man who had betrayed him. He had him immediately seized, and, putting a pistol to his head, bade him say his prayers, as he had only five minutes to live. The man did as he was desired, and perceiving that his death was resolved upon, calmly placed his head against the door of a hut by which they were standing, and, telling him to 'fire, and be d——d to him,' was immediately shot in the head. The body being left unburied, was soon afterwards discovered, when it was found that the bullet had scarcely penetrated the skull, and was as flat as a shilling. Shortly after this Radley was taken, and once more cast into prison.

About this time a plan had been adopted by the Government to endeavour to break up several gangs of bushrangers, which then infested the country and spread terror throughout the pastoral districts. It was, in fact, putting in practice the old adage: set a thief to catch a thief. Radley was an admirable person to be enlisted in this service, and as there was no evidence against him of his having committed the murder above recorded, his cunning and courage were immediately called into requisition to help in carrying out the plans of the authorities. It was suggested to him that he should become a man-decoy, and, under the pretence of having just escaped again from jail, retain his irons until he once more joined the bushrangers, whom he was then to betray into the hands of the Government. This scheme had already been put in practice, and had in several instances proved quite successful; but as the rangers had, from experience, now become awake to it, they were no longer to be the dupes of such an artifice. Radley, however, in the prospect of some mitigation of punishment, or, perhaps, in the hope of once more tasting the sweets of liberty, undertook the perfidious office, and, with his irons clanking around him, sallied forth on his enterprise.

As he was well acquainted with the haunts of the depredators, he soon encountered a gang, which he wished immediately to join. He told them who he was, and asserted that he had just escaped from prison; but as suspicion is the constant companion of a guilty mind, they believed him to have taken up the trade of a decoyer, and adjudged him to suffer death. Five minutes, however, were allowed him to make his peace with God; but as Radley could have very little to say for himself, even to man, in extenuation of his crimes, it may be fairly presumed that his mind was occupied with other speculations than such as were suitable to be addressed to a Supreme tribunal.

The brief time allowed him having expired, and he himself still manacled with the irons which he had carried from prison, he could offer no resistance, even if such would have availed him anything against a numerous body of ruffians, as determined as he was himself; he therefore had no alternative but to submit to a very disagreeable fate. He soon saw that he was not to be shot, but poisoned; for these worthies, acting upon the principles of some of the ancient philosophers, carried a quantity of laudanum with them for the purpose of putting themselves quietly to rest, in preference to being ignominiously sent out of the world with a halter about their necks, should it have been their misfortune to have been captured by the Government.

'You're surely never a-going to give me poison!' said Radley, as the rough executioner of bushranging justice approached with a bottleful of the draught in his hand.

'Only a sleeping-draught,' returned the other with a horrid smile, 'to carry you into the other world with no greater noise than your own snores.'

'I'd rather be shot,' said Radley, 'than die in that there sort of cowardly way. Put a bullet through my head, and that will do my trick equally well.'

'Waste powder and lead on a scoundrel like you!' exclaimed the captain of the gang; and uttering a terrible oath, told him to take his medicine, or he would relieve him from his irons, make him dig his own grave, and bury him alive. It is scarcely necessary to say that the prospect of such a death silenced all further expostulation on the part of Radley. He now swallowed a whole bottle of laudanum, fell to the ground, and in a few minutes was left for dead.

Whether it was from the quantity or the quality of the poison, Charlie could not say; but, at all events, Radley did not die. For shortly after the gang had quitted him, which they soon did, only waiting to bestow upon his carcass a hearty kick or two accompanied with a few curses, his stomach rejected the drug, the narcotic properties of which subjected him only to the pleasure of a sounder nap than he had for many years been in the habit of enjoying. When he awoke, he found himself still a man in irons, and scarcely could believe it possible that he was yet in the land of the living; and perhaps was at some difficulty to be assured of his identity and that he was not in the regions of the damned, where he certainly had expected to be long before this time. Gathering himself and his manacles together, however, he arose and moved off, communing with himself on the wisest course to pursue: to give himself up to the authorities again, narrate what had befallen him, and suggest some other mode of capturing the banditti, or try to fall in with his own gang and once more declare himself a bushranger.

Whilst revolving these ideas in his mind, and wandering in a direction hardly known to himself, he unfortunately fell in with the same party who so recently left him for dead.

'Hollo! What! arn't ye dead yet?' was the greeting which he received from him who had administered to him the potion which was supposed to have the virtue of death in a single mouthful. 'Well, we'll be able to cook your goose this time, at all events.'

For a few moments they held a consultation amongst themselves, portions of which were delivered in a voice and tone sufficiently audible to Radley, who, whatever might be his general regardlessness of death, had his own peculiar feelings as to the mode in which it was to be suffered.

'Flay the devil alive!' said one, whose low beetle-brow hung like a rock over a pair of small gloomy eyes, as remarkable for their malignity of expression as they were for the depth in which they were sunk in his head. 'Flay him alive, and salt the devil to preserve him in his agony,' said he, and smiled at the sport which the novelty of his own merciful idea, if carried out, would furnish to the fiendish crew with which he was associated.

'That would take too much time, and he's not worth it,' observed a more charitable friend, with a look at their victim sufficiently indicative of the unutterable contempt in which he was held.

'D——n him!' There's no death too hard for such a fellow,' said another; 'for he would have put the darbies on us all, if he could, and would have given us a hempen cravat for a comforter.'

'Let's pistol him at once,' said the captain. 'That's the surest and the shortest way of getting rid o' such a varmin.'

'Aye, aye!' cried two or three more, who drew their weapons from their belts, and examined the state of their locks.

'I say, my lad,' cried the captain, 'since you got five minutes for your prayers last time, you won't need such a favour this time; so there's a nut for you to crack on your way to hell'; and, discharging his pistol, struck him in the back. The ball, however, in place of wounding him vitally, passed around the surface of his body, and inflicted a wound only sufficiently severe to bring him to the ground as if in a lifeless state. Another pistol was discharged at him, but only gave a flesh-wound of no great magnitude. At this moment, the sound of some horses' footsteps passing along a bush-road disturbed these ministers of death in their work of blood, when they took to flight, leaving the account of Radley, as they supposed, sufficiently settled for this world. He, however, was not yet dead; and again gathering himself up, and moving off in the best manner he could, with the resolution of giving himself up, was so unfortunate as once more to meet with the same gang.

'Good Lord deliver us! Not dead yet!' was the astonished ejaculation of one of the myrmidons.

'He has as many lives as a cat!' cried another, whilst some more had their doubts as to his humanity; or at all events, believed that he bore, like Macbeth, a charmed existence. As they were now bent upon an enterprise of some importance, they had no time for delay, when one of them deliberately fired at Radley's head, and dropped him in an instant. The murderer looked over him for a moment, rudely turned over his body with his foot, at the same time saying, 'Your hash is settled at last,' then hastened with the rest upon their expedition.

Radley's hash was not yet settled, however, and his tenacity of life and the density of his skull were alike proved on the present occasion, for in place of being dead, he was, in reality, less injured than he had hitherto been. The fact was, that instead of the bullet perforating his skull, as it certainly would have done

one of ordinary thickness, it glanced and circulated nearly around it, making a severe wound, but only sufficient to strike him senseless to the ground. He was shortly afterwards found in this state, was carried to a hut, where he recovered of his wounds, was subsequently employed in several offices connected with the constabulary force, and lived for many years in the colony to tell the strange and almost incredible story of his adventures. The murder which he himself committed was never proved against him, and it is to be presumed that he was too wise a politician ever to give that a place in the history of his own career.

Such was the history which Charlie narrated as composed of nothing but fact, although it may be considered doubtful whether his own imagination and ingenuity did not add something to it by way of giving it a higher degree of colouring and dramatic effect; but whether this was the case or not, it brought round the hour of going to bed.

JOHN LANG

Fisher's Ghost

In Botany Bay, or True Stories of the Early Days of Australia, *first published in London in 1859, John Lang (c.1817–1864) retold some of the traditional stories of Australia that he had probably heard as a youth in Parramatta (NSW) and Sydney. The longest of these tales is 'Fisher's Ghost', which is here reprinted from a 1920 edition of the above-mentioned book, retitled* Fisher's Ghost and Other Stories of the Early Days of Australia.

It was a winter's night in the middle of July, when two wealthy farmers, in the district of Penrith, New South Wales, sat over the fire of a public-house, which was about a mile distant from their homes. The name of the one was John Fisher, and of the other Edward Smith. Both of these farmers had been transported to the colony; had served their time; bought land; cultivated it; and prospered. Fisher had the reputation of being possessed of a considerable sum in ready money; and it was well known that he was the mortgagee of several houses in the town of Sydney, besides being the owner of a farm of three hundred acres, which was very productive, and on which he lived. Smith also was in good circumstances; arising out of his own exertions on his farm; but, unlike his neighbour, he had not put by much money.

'Why don't you go home, John, and see your friends and re-lations?' asked Smith; 'you be now very warm in the pocket; and, mark my words, they would be very glad to see you.'

'I don't know about that, friend,' replied Fisher. 'When I got into trouble, it was the breaking of the heart of my old father and mother; and none of my brothers and sisters—in all seven of 'em—have ever answered one of my letters.'

'You did not tell 'em you were a rich man, did you?'

'No; but I don't think they would heed that much, lad; for though they are far from wealthy, as small farmers, they are well to do in the world, and in a very respectable position in the country. I have often thought that if I was to go back, they would be sorry to see me, even if I carried with me £100,000 earned by one who had been a convict.'

'Bless your innocent heart! You don't know human natur' as I do. Money does a deal—depend on't. Besides, who is to know anything about you, except your own family? And they would never go and hint that they had been unfortunate. Why, how many years ago is it?'

'Let me see. I was then eighteen, and I am forty-six—twenty-eight years ago. When I threw that stone at that man, I little thought it would hit him, much less kill him; and that I should be sent here for manslaughter. But so it was.'

'Why I recommend you, John, to go home, is because you are always talking of home and your relations. As for the farm, I'd manage that for you while you are away.'

'Thank you, Ned. I'll think about it.'

Presently the landlord entered the room, and Smith, addressing him, said, 'What think you, Mr Dean? Here is Mr Fisher going home to England to have a look at his friends and relations.'

'Is that true, Mr Fisher?' said the landlord.

'Oh, yes,' was Fisher's reply, after finishing his glass of punch, and knocking the ashes out of his pipe.

'And when do you think of going?' said the landlord.

'That'll depend,' replied Fisher, smiling. 'When I'm gone you will hear of it, not before; and neighbour Smith here, who is to manage the farm during my absence, will come and pay you any little score I may leave behind.'

'But I hope you will come and say good-bye,' said the landlord.

'Oh, of course,' said Fisher, laughing. 'If I don't, depend upon it you will know the reason why.'

After a brief while the two farmers took their departure. Their farms adjoined each other, and they were always on the very best of terms.

About six weeks after the conversation above given, Smith called one morning at the public-house, informed the landlord that Fisher had gone, and offered to pay any little sum that he owed. There was a small score against him; and while taking the money the landlord remarked that he was sorry Mr Fisher had not kept his word and come to bid him 'good-bye'. Mr Smith explained that Fisher had very good reasons for having his departure kept a secret until after he had left the colony; not that he wanted to defraud anybody, far from it, he added; and then darkly hinted that one of Mr Fisher's principal reasons for going off so stealthily was to prevent being annoyed by a woman who wanted him to marry her.

'Ah! I see,' said the landlord; 'and that's what he must have meant that night when he said, "if I don't, you'll hear the reason why".'

'I feel the loss of his society very much,' said Smith, 'for when we did not come here together to spend our evening, he would come to my house, or I would go to his, to play cards, smoke a pipe, and drink a glass of grog. Having taken charge of all his affairs, under a power of attorney, I have gone to live at his place, and left my overseer in charge of my own place. When he comes back, in the course of a couple of years, I am going home to England, and he will do for me what I am now doing for him. Between ourselves, Mr Dean, he has gone home to get a wife.'

'Indeed!' said the landlord. Here the conversation ended, and Mr Smith went home.

Fisher's sudden departure occasioned some surprise throughout the district; but when the explanation afforded by Mr Smith was spread abroad by Mr Dean, the landlord, people ceased to think any more about the matter.

A year elapsed, and Mr Smith gave out that he had received a letter from Fisher, in which he stated that it was not his intention to return to Sydney; and that he wished the whole of his property to be sold, and the proceeds remitted to him. This letter Mr Smith showed to several of Fisher's most intimate acquaintances, who regretted extremely that they would see no more of so good a neighbour and so worthy a man.

Acting on the power of attorney which he held, Mr Smith advertised the property for sale—the farm, the live stock, the farming implements, the furniture, etc., in the farmhouse, also some cottages and pieces of land in and near Sydney and Parramatta. With Fisher's mortgagors, also, he came to an agreement for the repayment, within a few months, of the sums due by them.

About a month previous to the day of sale, an old man, one David Weir, who farmed a small piece of land in the Penrith-road, and who took every week to the Sydney market, butter, eggs, fowls, and a few bushels of Indian maize, was returning to his home when he saw, seated on a rail, the well-known form of Mr Fisher. It was very dark, but the figure and the face were as plainly visible as possible. The old man, who was not drunk, though he had been drinking at Dean's public-house, pulled up and called out, 'Halloa, Mr Fisher! I thought you were at home in England?' There was no reply, and the old man, who was impatient to get home, as was his horse, loosed the reins and proceeded on his journey.

'Mother,' said old Weir to his wife, while she was helping him off with his old top-coat, 'I've seen either Mr Fisher or his ghost.'

'Nonsense!' cried the old woman; 'you could not have seen Mr Fisher, for he is in Old England; and as for spirits, you never see any without drinking them; and you are full of 'em now.'

'Do you mean to say I'm drunk, mother?'

'No; but I can see, and hear, and understand, and know what I am about.'

'Well, then, have your supper and go to bed; and take my advice, and say nothing to anybody about this ghost, or you will only get laughed at for your pains. Ghosts, indeed! at your age to take on about such things; after swearing all your life you never believed in them.'

'But I tell you I saw him as plain as plain could be; just as we used to see him sitting sometimes when the day was warm, and he had been round looking at his fences to see that they were all right.'

'Yes, very well; tell me all about it to-morrow,' said the old woman. 'As I was up before daylight, and it is now nearly midnight, I feel too tired to listen to a story about a ghost. Have you sold everything well?'

'Yes; and brought back all the money safely. Here it is.' The old man handed the bag over to his partner and retired to his bed; not to rest, however, for the vision had made so great an impression upon his mind he could not help thinking of it, and lay awake till daylight, when he arose, as did his wife, to go through the ordinary avocations of the day. After he had milked the cows, and brought the filled pails into the dairy, where the old woman was churning, she said to him:

'Well, David, what about the ghost?'

'I tell you I seed it,' said the old man. 'And there's no call for you to laugh at me. If Mr Fisher be not gone away—and I don't think he would have done so without coming to say goodbye to us—I'll make a talk of this. I'll go and tell Sir John, and Doctor Mackenzie, and Mr Cox, and old Parson Fulton, and everybody else in the commission of the peace. I will, as I'm a living man! What should take Fisher to England? England would be no home for him after being so many years in this country. And, what's more, he has told me as much many a time.'

'Well, and so he has told me, David. But then, you know, people will alter their minds, and you heard what Mr Smith said about that woman?'

'Yes. But I don't believe Smith. I never had a good opinion of that man, for he could never look me straight in the face, and he is too oily a character to please me. If, as I tell you, Mr Fisher is not alive in this country, then that was his ghost that I saw, and he has been murdered!'

'Be careful, David, what you say; and whatever you do, don't offend Mr Smith. Remember, he is a rich man, and you are a poor one; and if you say a word to his discredit, he may take the law of you, and make you pay for it; and that would be a pretty business for people who are striving to lay by just enough to keep them when they are no longer able to work.'

'There's been foul play, I tell you, old woman. I am certain of it.'

'But that can't be proved by your saying that you saw a ghost sitting on a rail, when you were coming home from market none the better for what you drank upon the road. And if Mr Fisher should still be alive in England—and you know that letters have been lately received from him—what a precious fool you would look!'

'Well, perhaps you are right. But when I tell you that I saw either Mr Fisher or his ghost sitting on that rail, don't laugh at me, because you will make me angry.'

'Well, I won't laugh at you, though it must have been your fancy, old man. Whereabouts was it you saw, or thought you saw him?'

'You know the cross fence that divides Fisher's land from Smith's—near the old bridge, at the bottom of Iron Gang Hill?'

'Yes.'

'Well, it was there; I'll tell you what he was dressed in. You know that old fustian coat, with the brass buttons, and the corduroy waistcoat and trousers, and that red silk bandanna handkerchief that he used to tie around his neck?'

'Yes.'

'Well, that's how he was dressed. His straw hat he held in his left hand, and his right arm was resting on one of the posts. I was about ten or eleven yards from him, for the road is broad just there, and the fence stands well back.'

'And you called him, you say?'

'Yes; but he did not answer. If the horse had not been so fidgety, I'd have got down and gone up to him.'

'And then you would have found out that it was all smoke.'

'Say that again, and you will put me into a passion'.

The old woman held her tongue, and suffered old David to talk all that day and the next about the ghost, without making any remark whatever.

On the following Wednesday—Thursday being the market-day in Sydney—old David Weir loaded his cart, and made his way to the Australian metropolis. True to his word with his wife, he did not mention to a soul one syllable touching the ghost. Having disposed of his butter, eggs, poultry and maize, the old man left Sydney at four p.m., and, at half-past ten, arrived at Dean's public-house.

He had travelled in that space of time thirty miles, and was now about eight or nine from home. As was his wont, he here baited the horse; but declined taking any refreshment himself, though pressed to do so by several travellers who wanted to 'treat' him. During the whole day he had been remarkably abstemious.

At a quarter to twelve the old man re-harnessed his jaded horse, and was about to resume his journey, when two men, who were going to Penrith, asked him for a 'lift'.

'Jump up, my lads,' said old David; and off they were driven at a brisk walk. One of the men in the cart was a ticket-of-leave man in the employ of Mr Cox, and had been to Sydney to attend 'muster'. The other was a newly-appointed constable of the district. Both of these men had lived for several years in the vicinity of Penrith, and knew by sight all the inhabitants, male and female, free and bond.

When they neared the spot where the old man had seen the apparition, he walked the horse as slowly as possible, and again beheld the figure of Mr Fisher, seated on the upper rail of the fence, and in precisely the same attitude and the same dress.

'Look there!' said old David to the two men, 'What is that?'

'It is a man!' they both replied; 'but how odd! It seems as if a light were shining through him!'

'Yes,' said old David; 'but look at him. What man is it?'

'It is Mr Fisher,' they said, simultaneously.

'Hold the reins, one of you,' said old David; 'I'll go and speak to him. They say he is at home in England; but I don't believe it.'

Descending from the cart, the old man, who was as brave as a lion, approached the spectre, and stood within a few feet of it. 'Speak!' he cried; 'don't you know me, sire? I am David Weir. How came you by that gash in your forehead? Are you alive or dead, Mr Fisher?' To these questions no answer was returned. The old man then stretched forth his hand and placed it on what appeared to be Mr Fisher's shoulder; but it was only empty air, vacant space, that the intended touch rested upon!

'There has been foul play!' said the old man, addressing the spectre, but speaking sufficiently loud to be heard by both men in the cart. 'And, by heaven, it shall be brought to light! Let me mark the spot', and with these words he broke off several boughs from a tree near the rail, and placed them opposite to where the spectre remained sitting. Nay, further, he took out his clasp knife, and notched the very part on which the right hand of the spectre rested.

Even after the old man returned to the cart, the apparition of Mr Fisher, exactly as he was in the flesh, was 'palpable to the sight' of all three men. They sat gazing at it for full ten minutes, and then drove on in awe and wonderment.

When old David Weir arrived at home, his wife, who was delighted to see him so calm and collected, inquired, laughingly, if he had seen the ghost again. 'Never mind about that,' said the old man. 'Here, take the money, and lock it up, while I take the horse out of the cart. He is very tired, and no wonder, for the roads are nearly a foot deep in dust. This is the fifteenth month that has passed since we had the last shower of rain; but never mind! If it holds off for a fortnight or three weeks longer, our maize will be worth thirty shillings a bushel. It is wrong to grumble at the ways of Providence. In my belief it is very wicked.'

'Well, I think so, too,' said the old woman. 'Thirty shillings a bushel! Why, Lord a bless us, that'll set us up in the world, surely! What a mercy we did not sell when it rose to nine and sixpence!'

'Get me some supper ready, for as soon as I have taken it, I have some business to transact.'

'Not out of the house?'

'Never you mind. Do as I tell you.'

Having eaten his supper, the old man rose from his chair, put on his hat, and left his abode. In reply to his wife's question, 'Where are you going?' he said, 'To Mr Cox's; I'll be home in an hour or so. I have business, as I told you, to transact.'

The old woman suggested that he could surely wait till the morning; but he took no heed of her, and walked away.

Mr Cox was a gentleman of very large property in the district, and was one of the most zealous and active magistrates in the colony. At all times of the day or night he was accessible to any person who considered they had business with him.

It was past two o'clock in the morning when David Weir arrived at Mr Cox's house, and informed the watchman that he desired to see the master. It was not the first time that the old man had visited Mr Cox at such an hour. Two years previously he had been plundered by bushrangers, and, as soon as they had gone, he went to give the information.

Mr Cox came out, received the old man very graciously, and invited him to enter the house. Old David followed the magistrate, and detailed all that the reader is in possession of touching the ghost of Mr Fisher.

'And who were with you,' said Mr Cox, 'on the second occasion of your seeing this ghost?'

'One is a ticket-of-leave man, named Williams, a man in your own employ; and the other was a man named Hamilton, who lived for several years with Sir John Jamieson. They both rode with me in my cart,' was the old man's answer.

'Has Williams returned?'

'Yes, sir.'

'It is very late, and the man may be tired and have gone to bed; but, nevertheless, I will send for him.' And Mr Cox gave the order for Williams to be summoned.

Williams in a few minutes came, and corroborated David Weir's statement in every particular.

'It is the most extraordinary thing I ever heard in my life,' said Mr Cox. 'But go home, Weir, and you, Williams, go to your rest. To-morrow morning I will go with you to the spot and examine it. You say that you have marked it, Weir?'

'Yes, sir.'

The old man then left Mr Cox, and Williams returned to his hut. Mr Cox did not sleep again till a few minutes before the day dawned, and then, when he dropped off for a quarter of an hour, he dreamt of nothing but the ghost sitting on the rail.

The next morning, or rather on that morning, Mr Cox, at eight o'clock, rode over to the township of Penrith, and saw Hamilton, Weir's second witness. Hamilton, as did Williams, corroborated all that Weir had stated, so far as related to the second time the spectre had been seen; and Hamilton further volunteered the assertion that no one of the party was in the slightest degree affected by drink.

There was a tribe of blacks in the vicinity, and Mr Cox sent for the chief and several others. The European name of this chief was 'Johnny Crook', and, like all his race, was an adept in tracking. Accompanied by Weir, Hamilton, Williams and the blacks, Mr Cox proceeded to the spot. Weir had no difficulty in pointing out the exact rail. The broken boughs and the notches on the post were his unerring guides.

Johnny Crook, after examining the rail very minutely, pointed to some stains, and exclaimed, 'White man's blood!' Then, leaping over the fence, he examined the brushwood and the ground adjacent. Ere long he started off, beckoning Mr Cox and his attendants to follow. For more than three-quarters of a mile, over

forest land, the savage tracked the footsteps of a man, and something trailed along the earth (fortunately, so far as the ends of
justice were concerned, no rain had fallen during the period
alluded to by old David, namely, fifteen months. One heavy
shower would have obliterated all these tracks, most probably;
and, curious enough, that very night there was a frightful downfall, such a downfall as had not been known for many a long
year), until they came to a pond, or waterhole, upon the surface
of which was a bluish scum. This scum the blacks, after an
examination of it, declared to be 'white man's fat'. The pond in
question was not on Fisher's land, or Smith's. It was on Crown
land, in the rear of their properties. When full to the brink, the
depth of the water was about ten feet in the centre; but at the
time referred to there was not more than three feet and a-half,
and badly as the cattle wanted water, it was evident, from the
absence of recent hock-prints, that they would not drink at this
pond. The blacks walked into the water at the request of Mr Cox,
and felt about the muddy bottom with their feet. They were not
long employed thus, when they came upon a bag of bones, or,
rather, the remains of a human body, kept together by clothing,
which had become so rotten it would scarcely bear the touch.
The skull was still attached to the body, which the blacks raised
to the surface and brought on shore, together with a big stone,
and the remains of a large silk handkerchief. The features were
not recognizable, but the buttons on the clothes, and the boots,
were those which Mr Fisher used to wear! And in the pocket
of the trousers was found a buckhorn-handled knife, which bore
the initials, 'J. F.', engraved on a small silver plate. This was
also identified by Weir, who had seen Mr Fisher use the knife
scores of times. It was one of those knives which contained a
large blade, two small ones, a corkscrew, gimlet, horse-shoe
picker, tweezers, screw-driver, & c., & c. The murderer, whoever it might be, had either forgotten to take away this knife,
or had purposely left it with the body, for all the other pockets
were turned inside out.

'Well, sir, what do you think of that?' said old Weir to Mr
Cox, who looked on in a state of amazement which almost
amounted to bewilderment.

'I scarcely know what to think of it,' was Mr Cox's reply. 'But
it is lucky for you, David, that you are a man of such good

character that you are beyond the pale of being suspected of so foul a deed.'

'I, sir?'

'Yes, you. If it were not that this dead man's property is advertised for sale, it might have gone very hard with you, old man. It would have been suggested that your conscience had something to do with the information you gave me of the ghost. But stay here, all of you, with the body until I return. I shall not be absent for more than an hour. Have you a pair of handcuffs about you, Hamilton?'

'Several pairs, sir,' replied the constable.

After leaving the dead body, Mr Cox rode to Fisher's house, in which Mr Smith was living. Mr Smith, on being informed of the approach of so exalted a person as Mr Cox, one of the proudest men in the colony, came out to receive him with all respect and honour. Mr Cox—who would not have given his hand to an 'expiree' (under any circumstances), no matter how wealthy he might be—answered Mr Smith's greeting with a bow, and then asked if he could speak with him for a few minutes. Mr Smith replied, 'Most certainly, sir'; and ordering a servant to take the magistrate's horse to the stables, he conducted his visitor into the best room of the weather-boarded and comfortable tenement. The furniture was plain and homely, but comfortable, nevertheless, and remarkably clean. The pictures on the walls formed rather a motley collection, having been picked up at various times by Mr Fisher at sales by public auction of the effects of deceased officials. Amongst others were two valuable oil-paintings, which had originally belonged to Major Ovens, an eccentric officer, who was buried on Garden Island, in the harbour of Port Jackson. These had been bought for less money than the frames were worth. There were also some Dutch paintings, of which neither Mr Fisher nor those who had not bid against him knew the real value when they were knocked down for forty-two shillings the set—six in number!

'I have come to speak to you on a matter of business,' said the magistrate. 'Is the sale of this farm and the stock to be a peremptory sale?—that is to say, will it be knocked down, bona fide, to the highest bidder?'

'Yes, sir.'

'And the terms are cash?'

'Yes, sir.'

'Sales for cash are not very common in this country. The terms are usually ten per cent deposit, and the residue at three, six, nine, and twelve months, in equal payments.'

'Very true, sir; but these are Mr Fisher's instructions, by which I must be guided.'

'What do you imagine the farm will realize, including the stock and all that is upon it?'

'Well, sir, it ought to fetch £1,500, ready money.'

'I hear that the whole of Mr Fisher's property is to be sold, either by auction or private contract.'

'Yes, sir.'

'What will it realize, think you, in cash?'

'Not under £12,000, I should say, sir.'

'One of my brothers has an idea of bidding for this farm: what about the title?'

'As good as can be, sir. It was originally granted to Colonel Foucaux, who sold it and conveyed it to Mr Thomas Blaxsell, who sold it and conveyed it to Fisher. But, as you know, sir, twenty years undisputed possession of itself makes a good title, and Fisher has been on this farm far longer than that. All the deeds are here; you may see them, if you please, sir.'

'There is no occasion for that; as Mr Fisher's constituted attorney, you will sign the deed of conveyance on his behalf.'

'Yes, sir.'

'What is the date of the power of attorney?'

'I will tell you, sir, in one moment;' and, opening a bureau which stood in one corner of the room, Mr Smith produced the deed, and placed it in Mr Cox's hands.

With the signature of Fisher, Mr Cox was not acquainted; or, at all events, he could not swear to it. He had seen it—seen Fisher write his name, it is true; but, then, it was that sort of hand which all uneducated and out-door working-men employ when they write their names—a sprawling round-hand. But as to the signatures of the attesting witnesses, there could be no question whatever. They were those of two of the most eminent solicitors (partners) in Sydney—Mr Cox's own solicitors, in fact.

'And the letter of instruction, authorizing you to sell by auction, for cash; for it says in this power, "and to sell the same, or any part thereof, in accordance with such instructions as he may receive from me by letter after my arrival in England." '

'Here is the letter, sir,' said Mr Smith, producing it.

Mr Cox read the letter attentively. It ran thus:

> Dear Sir, —I got home all right, and found my friends and relations quite well and hearty, and very glad to see me again. I am so happy among 'em, I shan't go out no more to the colony. So sell all off, by public auction, or by private contract, but let it be for cash, as I want the money sharp; I am going to buy a share in a brewery with it. I reckon it ought, altogether, to fetch about £17,000. But do your best, and let me have it quick, whatever it is.
>
> Your faithful friend,
JOHN FISHER.

There was no post-mark on this letter. In those days the postage on letters was very high, and nothing was more common for persons in all conditions of life to forward communications by private hand. As to the signature of the letter, it was identical with that of the power of attorney.

'All this is very satisfactory,' said Mr Cox. 'Is this letter, dated five months ago, the last you have received?'

'Yes, sir. It came by the last ship, and there has not been another in since.'

'Good-morning, Mr Smith.'

'Good-morning, sir.'

Riding away from Fisher's late abode, Mr Cox was somewhat perplexed. That power of attorney, drawn up so formally, and signed by Fisher in the presence of such credible witnesses, and then the letter written, signed in the same way by the same hand, were all in favour of the presumption that Fisher had gone to England, leaving his friend and neighbour Smith in charge of his property, real and personal. But then, there were the remains! And that they were the remains of Fisher, Mr Cox firmly believed. When he had returned to the pond, by a circuitous route, Mr Cox ordered the blacks to strip from a blue-gum tree, with their tomahawks, a large sheet of bark. Upon this the remains were placed, carried straightway to Fisher's house (Mr Cox, upon horseback, heading the party), and placed in the verandah.

While this proceeding was in progress, Mr Smith came out, and wore upon his countenance an expression of surprise, astonishment, wonder. But there was nothing in that. The most innocent man in the world would be surprised, astonished, and in wonderment on beholding such a spectacle.

'What is this, Mr Cox?' he said.

'The last that I have heard and seen of Mr Fisher,' was the reply.

'Of Mr Fisher, sir!'

'Yes.'

'These were his old clothes,' said Mr Smith, examining them carefully: 'most certainly this was the old suit he used to wear. But as for the body, it can't be his; for he is alive, as you have seen by his letter. These old clothes he must have given away, as he did many other old things, the day before he left this, and the man to whom he gave 'em must have been murdered.'

'Do you think he could have given away this knife?' said David Weir. 'To my knowledge, he had it for better than twelve years, and often have I heard him say he would not part with it for £50.'

'Give it away? Yes!' said Smith. 'Didn't he give away his old saddle and bridle? Didn't he give away his old spurs? Didn't he give away a cow and a calf?'

'He was a good man, and an honest man, and a very fair-dealing man, and in his latter days a very righteous and godly man; but he was not a giving-away man by any manner of means,' returned old David.

'And if he gave away these boots,' said Hamilton, 'they were a very good fit for the man who received them.'

'This man, whoever he is, was murdered, no doubt,' said Mr Smith, with the most imperturbable countenance and the coolest manner. 'Just look at this crack in his skull, Mr Cox.'

'Yes, I have seen that,' said the magistrate.

'And that's where poor Fisher's ghost had it,' said old David.

'Fisher's ghost!' said Mr Smith. 'What do you mean, Weir?'

'Why, the ghost that I have seen sitting on the rail not far from the old bridge at the bottom of the hill yonder.'

'Ghost! you have seen a ghost, have you?' returned Mr Smith, giving Mr Cox a very cunning and expressive look.

'Well, I have heard that ghosts do visit those who have sent them out of this world, and I dare say Mr Cox has heard the same. Now, if I had been you, I'd have held my tongue about a ghost (for ghosts are only the creatures of our conscience) for fear of being taken in charge.'

'I taken in charge!' said old Weir. 'No, no! my conscience is clear, and what I have seen and said I'll swear to. Wherever I go, I'll talk about it up to my dying hour. That was the ghost of Mr Fisher that I saw, and these are the remains of his body.'

'If I were Mr Cox, a magistrate,' said Mr Smith, 'I would give you in charge.'

'I will not do that, Mr Smith,' replied Mr Cox. 'I feel that my duty compels me to give you in custody of this police-officer.'

'For what, sir?'

'On a charge of wilful murder. Hamilton!'

'Yes, sir.'

'Manacle Mr Smith, and take him to Penrith.'

Mr Smith held up his wrists with the air of an injured and pure-minded man, who was so satisfied of his innocence that he was prepared for the strictest investigation into his conduct, and had no dread as to the result.

A coroner's inquest was held on the remains found in the pond, and a verdict of 'Wilful Murder' was returned against Edward Smith. The jury also found that the remains were those of John Fisher, albeit, they were so frightfully decomposed that personal identification was out of all question.

The vessel in which Fisher was reported to have left Sydney happened to be in the harbour. The captain and officers were interrogated, and in reply to the question—'Did a man named John Fisher go home in your vessel?'—the reply was, 'Yes, and on the Custom-house officers coming on board, as usual, to look at the passengers and search the ship, to see that no convicts were attempting to make their escape, he produced his parchment cer-tificate of freedom, in which there was a description of his per-son.'

'And did the man answer exactly to that description?'

'Yes, making allowance for his years, on looking at the date of the certificate. If he had not, he would have been detained, as many convicts have been.'

'And, during the voyage, did he talk of himself?'

'Frequently; he said that he was a farmer near Penrith; that, after he had served his time, he went to work, earned some money, rented a farm, then bought it, and by industry and perseverance had made a fortune.'

'Did he ever mention a Mr Smith—a friend of his?'

'Often. He said he had left everything in Mr Smith's hands, and that he did not like to sell his property till he saw how he should like England after so long an absence. He further said that if he did not come back to the colony, he would have all his property sold off, and join some trading firm in his own country.'

The solicitor who had prepared the power of attorney, and witnessed it, said that a person representing himself as John Fisher of Ruskdale, in the district of Penrith, came to them and gave instructions for the deed; and, after it was duly executed, took it away with him, and requested that a copy might be made and kept in their office, which was done accordingly. In payment of the bill, twenty dollars (£5 currency), he gave a cheque on the bank of New South Wales, which was cashed on presentation; that the man who so represented himself as John Fisher was a man of about forty-six or forty-eight years of age, about five feet eight inches in height, and rather stout; had light-blue eyes, sandy hair, and whiskers partially grey, a low but intelligent forehead, and a rather reddish nose.

This description answered exactly that of Mr Fisher at the time of his departure from the colony.

The cashier of the bank showed the cheque for twenty dollars. Mr Fisher had an account there, and drew out his balance, £200 (not in person, but by a cheque) two days previous to his alleged departure. He had written several letters to the bank, and on comparing those letters with the letter Mr Smith said he had received from England, they corresponded exactly.

Opinion was very much divided in the colony with respect to Mr Smith's guilt. Numbers of persons who knew the man, and had dealings with him, thought him incapable of committing such a crime, or any heinous offence, in fact. The records were looked into, to ascertain of what offence he had been convicted

originally. It was for embezzling the sum of twenty-two shillings
and fourpence, which had been entrusted to him when he was
an apprentice for his master, who was a market-gardener, seeds-
man, and florist. As for the story about the ghost, very, very few
put any trust in it. Bulwer was then a very young gentleman,
and had never dreamt of writing about Eugene Aram; nor had
Thomas Hood contemplated his exquisite little poem on the
subject. Nor had the murder of the Red Barn been brought to
light through the agency of a dream. The only instance of ghosts
coming to give evidence of murder were those of Banquo and
Hamlet's father; and Shakespeare was not considered an authority to be relied upon in such a case as that of Fisher.

Smith's house and premises, as well as those of Fisher, were
searched in the hope of finding apparel, or some garment stained
with blood, but in vain. Nor did the inspection of Smith's letters
and papers disclose aught that strengthened the case against him.
On the contrary, his accounts touching Fisher's property were
kept entirely distinct from his own; and in memorandum-books
were found entries of the following description:

Sept. 9. Wrote to Fisher to say P. has paid the interest on his
mortgage.

Sept. 27. Received £27/10/- from Wilson for year's rent of
fisher's house in Castlereagh-street.

Nov. 12. Paid Baxter £3/12/- due to him by Fisher for Bullock Chains.

No case had ever before created and probably never will again
create, so great a sensation. Very many were firmly impressed
with the belief that Weir was the murderer of the man who wore
Fisher's clothes, crediting Smith's assertion or suggestion that
he had given them away. Many others were of opinion that the
remains were those of Fisher, and the man who murdered him
had robbed him of his certificate of freedom, as well as of the
cash and papers he had about him, and then, representing Fisher,
had got out of the colony, and made Smith a dupe.

The anxiously-looked-for day of trial came. The court was
crowded with persons in every grade of society, from the highest
to the very lowest. Mr Smith stood in the dock as firmly and
as composedly as though he had been arraigned for a mere libel,
or a common assault—the penalty of conviction not exceeding

a fine and a few months' imprisonment.

The case was opened by the Attorney-General with the greatest fairness imaginable, and when the witnesses gave their evidence (Weir, Hamilton, Williams, and Mr Cox), everyone appeared to hold his breath. Smith, who defended himself, cross-examined them all with wonderful tact and ability; and, at the conclusion of the case for the prosecution, addressed the jury at considerable length, and with no mean amount of eloquence.

The judge then summed up. His Honour was the last man in the world to believe in supernatural appearances; but, with the ability and fairness that characterized his career in the colony, he weighed the probabilities and improbabilities with the greatest nicety. To detail all the points taken by the judge would be tedious; but if his charge had any leaning one way or other, it was in favour of the prisoner.

The jury in those days was not composed of the people, but of military officers belonging to the regiment quartered in the colony. These gentlemen, in ordinary cases, did not give much of their minds to the point at issue. Some of them usually threw themselves back, and shut their eyes—not to think, but 'nod'. Others whispered to each other, not about the guilt or innocence of the prisoner at the bar, but about their own affairs; whilst those who had any talent for drawing, exercised it by sketching the scene, or taking the likeness of the prisoner, the witnesses, the counsel, the sheriff, and the judge. But in this case they seemingly devoted all their energies, in order to enable them to arrive at the truth. To every word that fell from the judge during his charge, which lasted over two hours, they listened with breathless attention, and when it was concluded, they requested permission to retire to consider their verdict. This was at half-past five in the afternoon of Friday, and not until a quarter to eleven did the jury return into court and retake their places in the box.

The excitement that prevailed was intense, and when the murmurs in the crowd, so common upon such occasions, had subsided, amidst awful stillness the prothonotary put that all-momentous question, 'Gentlemen of the jury, what say you? Is the prisoner at the bar guilty, or not guilty?'

With a firm, clear voice, the foreman, a captain in the army, uttered the word: 'GUILTY!'

Murmurs of applause from some, and of disapprobation from others, instantly resounded through the hall of justice. From the reluctant manner in which the judge put the black cap upon his head, it was evident that he was not altogether satisfied with the finding of the jury. He had, however, no alternative; and in the usual formal manner, he sentenced the prisoner to be hanged on the following Monday morning, at eight o'clock.

Smith heard the sentence without moving a single muscle, or betraying any species of emotion, and left the dock with as firm a step as that which he employed when entering it. His demeanour throughout the trial, and after he was sentenced, brought over many who previously thought him guilty to a belief of his innocence, and a petition to the governor to spare his life was speedily drafted and numerously signed. It was rumoured that the chief justice, who tried the case, had also made a similar recommendation, and that the governor, in deference thereto, had ordered a reprieve to be made out; but not to be delivered to the sheriff until seven o'clock on Monday morning. It was further stated that the governor was of opinion that the finding of the jury was a correct one. The press of the colony did not lead, but fell into, the most popular opinion, that it would be tantamount to murder to take away the life of any human being upon such evidence as that given on the trial.

On the Monday morning, so early as half-past six, the rocks which overlooked the jail-yard in Sydney, and commanded a good view of the gallows, were crowded with persons of the lower orders; and when, at a little before seven, the hangman came out to suspend the rope to the beam, and make other preparations, he was hailed with loud hisses and execrations: so emphatic was the demonstration of the multitude in favour of the condemned man. By seven o'clock the mob was doubled; and when the under-sheriff or any other functionary was seen in the court-yard, the yells with which he was greeted were something terrific.

At five minutes to eight, the culprit was led forth, and at the foot of the gallows, and near his coffin (according to the custom prevailing in the colony), was pinioned, preparatory to ascending the ladder. Whilst this ceremony was being performed, the shouts of the populace were deafening. 'Shame! Shame! Shame! Hang Weir! He is the guilty man! This is a murder. A horrid murder!' Such were the ejaculations that resounded from every quarter of that dense mob assembled to witness the execution; while the calm and submissive manner in which Smith listened to the reverend gentleman, who attended him in his last moments, heightened rather than suppressed the popular clamour.

At one minute past eight the fatal bolt was drawn, and Smith, after struggling for about half a minute, was dead! Whereupon the mob renewed their yells, execrations, hisses, and cries of 'Shame! Shame! Shame! Murder! Murder! Murder!' These noises could not recall to life Mr Smith. He had gone to his account, and after hanging an hour, his body was cut down; the coffin containing it conveyed, in an uncovered cart, to Slaughter-House Point (the last resting-place of all great criminals), and the grave filled in with quicklime.

There was a gloom over Sydney until the evening at half-past six o'clock. Almost everyone was now disposed to think that the blood of an innocent man had been shed. 'The witnesses were all perjured, not excepting Mr Cox'; 'The jury were a parcel of fools'; and 'The Governor, who would not listen to the judge, a hard-hearted and cruel man.' Such were the opinions that were current from one end of Sydney to the other. But at the hour above mentioned—half-past six in the evening—the public mind was disabused of its erroneous idea. At that hour it became generally known that on the previous night Mr Smith had sent for the Rev. Mr Cooper, and to that gentleman had confessed that he deserved the fate that awaited him; that for more than two years he had contemplated the murder of John Fisher for the sake of his wealth, which was equal to £20,000; that the man who had personated Fisher, and executed the power of attorney, had gone to England, and written thence the letter upon which he so much relied in his defence, was a convict who resembled the deceased in person, and to whom he (Smith) gave Fisher's certificate of freedom; that it was his (Smith's) intention to have left the colony as soon as the proceeds of the sale came into his possession—partly because he longed to lead the last portion of his life in England, but chiefly because, from the day on which he committed the murder, he had been haunted by that ghost which old Weir had truly sworn he saw sitting on the rail; that the deed was done by a single blow from a tomahawk, and that the deceased never spoke after it was inflicted. He protested that the man who had personated Fisher, in respect to the execution of the power of attorney, and who had escaped from the colony, was ignorant of his (Smith's) intention to murder Fisher; and that the letter which had been forwarded from England was only a copy of one which he (Smith) had told him to despatch a few months after he had arrived at home. He concluded by saying, that since he struck Fisher that fatal blow his life had been a burden to him, much as he had struggled to disguise his feelings and put a bold front on the matter; and that he would much rather, since he had been convicted, suffer death than be reprieved—although he hoped that until after the breath had left his body, his confession would be kept a secret.

JOHN LANG

Barrington

From Botany Bay, or True Stories of the Early Days of Australia *(1859).*

George Barrington (1755–1804) was the 'con man' par excellence. Known as the 'Prince of Pickpockets', this Irish-born adventurer was sent as a convict to New South Wales, where he died. In Australia, as in England, he was the subject of several anecdotes highlighting his steady nerve and skill as a robber.

Suggested further reading: Bill Wannan, Legendary Australians *(1974).*

A few years ago I made the acquaintance of an elderly lady, whose husband, so far back as 1799, held an official position, both civil and military, in the colony of New South Wales. Many anecdotes she told me of celebrated characters who had, in the words of one of them, 'left their country for their country's good'. With most, if not with all, of these celebrities the old lady had come in contact personally.

'One morning,' she began, 'I was sitting in my drawing-room with my two little children, who are now middle-aged men with large families, when a gentleman was announced. I gave the order for his admission; and on his entering the door of the apartment, I rose from my chair, and greeted him with a bow, which he returned in the most graceful and courtly bow imaginable. His dress was that of a man of fashion, and his bearing that of a person who had moved in the highest circles of society. A vessel had arrived from England a few days previously with passengers, and I fancied that this gentleman was one of them. I asked him to be seated. He took a chair, opposite to me, and at once entered into conversation, making the first topic the extreme warmth of the day, and the second the healthful appearance of my charming children—as he was pleased to speak of them. Apart from a mother liking to hear her children praised, there was such a refinement in the stranger's manner, such a seeming sincerity in all he said, added to such a marvellous neatness of expression, that I could not help thinking he would form a very valuable acquisition to our list of acquaintances, provided he intended remaining in Sydney, instead of settling in the interior of the colony.

'I expressed my regret that the major (my husband) was away from home; but I mentioned that I expected him at one o'clock, at which hour we took luncheon; and I further expressed a hope that our visitor would remain and partake of the meal. With a very pretty smile (which I afterwards discovered had more meaning in it that I was at the time aware of), he feared he could not have the pleasure of partaking of the hospitalities of my table, but, with my permission, he would wait till the appointed hour, which was then near at hand. Our conversation was resumed; and presently he asked my little ones to go to him. They obeyed at once, albeit they were rather shy children. This satisfied me that the stranger was a man of a kind and gentle disposition. He took the children, seated them on his knees, and began to tell them a fairy story (evidently of his own invention, and extemporized), to which they listened with profound attention. Indeed, I could not help being interested in the story, so fanciful were the ideas, and so poetical the language in which they were expressed.

'The story ended, the stranger replaced the children on the carpet, and approached the table on which stood, in a porcelain vase, a bouquet of flowers. These he admired, and began a discourse of floriculture. I listened with intense earnestness; so profound were all his observations. We were standing at the table for at least eight or ten minutes; my boys hanging on to the skirt of my dress, and every now and then compelling me to beg of them to be silent.

'One o'clock came, but not the major. I received, however, a note from him, written in pencil on a slip of paper. He would be detained at Government House until half-past two.

'Again I requested the fascinating stranger to partake of luncheon, which was now on the table in the next room; and again, with the same winning smile, he declined. As he was about, as I thought, to depart, I extended my hand; but, to my astonishment, he stepped back, made a low bow, and declined taking it.

'For a gentleman to have his hand refused when he extends it to another is embarrassing enough. But for a lady! Who can possibly describe what were my feelings? Had he been the heir to the British throne, visiting that penal settlement in disguise (and from the stranger's manners and conversation he might have been that illustrious personage), he could scarcely have, under the circumstances, treated me in such an extraordinary manner. I scarcely knew what to think. Observing, as the stranger must have done, the blood rush to my cheeks, and being cognisant evidently of what was passing through my mind, he spoke as follows:

' "Madam, I am afraid you will never forgive me the liberty I have taken already. But the truth is, the passion suddenly stole over me, and I could not resist the temptation of satisfying myself that the skill which made me so conspicuous in the mother country still remained to me in this convict land."

' "Madam," he continued, "the penalty of sitting at table with you, or taking the hand you paid me the compliment to proffer me—yourself in ignorance of the fact I am about to disclose— would have been the forfeiture of my ticket-of-leave, a hundred lashes, and employment on the roads in irons. As it is, I dread the major's wrath; but I cherish a hope that you will endeavour to appease it, if your advocacy be only a return for the brief amusement I afforded your beautiful children."

' "You are a convict!" I said, indignantly, my hand on the bell-rope.

' "Madam," he said, with an expression of countenance which moved me to pity, in spite of my indignation, "hear me for one moment."

' "A convicted felon, how dare you enter my drawing-room as a visitor?" I asked him, my anger again getting the better of all my other feelings.

' "The major, madam," said the stranger, "requested me to be at his house at the hour when I presented myself; and he bade me wait if he were from home when I called. The major wishes to know who was the person who received from me a diamond necklace which belonged to the Marchioness of Dorrington, and came into my possession at a state ball some four or five years ago—a state ball at which I had the honour of being present. Now, madam, when the orderly who opened the front door informed me that the major was not at home, but that you were, that indomitable impudence which so often carried me into the drawing-rooms of the aristocracy of our country, took possession of me; and, warmed as I was with generous wine—just sufficient to give me courage—I determined to tread once more on a lady's carpet, and enter into conversation with her. That much I felt the major would forgive me; and, therefore, I requested the orderly to announce a gentleman. Indeed, madam, I shall make the forgiveness of the liberties I have taken in this room the condition of my giving that information which shall restore to the Marchioness of Dorrington the gem of which I deprived her—a gem which is still unpledged, and in the possession of one who will restore it on an application, accompanied by a letter in my handwriting."

'Again I kept silence.

' "Madam!" he exclaimed, somewhat impassionedly, and rather proudly, "I am no other man than Barrington, the illustrious pickpocket; and this is the hand which in its day has gently plucked, from ladies of rank and wealth, jewels which realized, in all, upwards of thirty-five thousand pounds, irrespective of those which were in my possession, under lock and key, when fortune turned her back upon me."

' "Barrington, the pickpocket!" Having heard so much of this man and of his exploits (although, of course, I had never seen him), I could not help regarding him with curiosity; so much so, that I could scarcely be angry with him any longer.

' "Madam," he continued, "I have told you that I longed to satisfy myself whether that skill which rendered me so illustrious in Europe still remained to me, in this country, after five years of desuetude. I can conscientiously say that I am just as perfect in the art; that the touch is just as soft, and the nerve as steady as when I sat in the dress circle at Drury Lane or Covent Garden."

' "I do not comprehend you, Mr Barrington," I replied. (I could not help saying "Mister".)

' "But you will, madam, in one moment. Where are your keys?"

'I felt in my pocket, in which I fancied they were, and discovered that they were gone.

' "And your thimble and pencil-case, and your smelling-salts? They are here!" (He drew them from his coat pocket.)

'My anger was again aroused. It was indeed, I thought, a frightful liberty for a convict to practise his skills upon me, and put his hand into the pocket of my dress. But, before I could request him to leave the room and the house, he spoke again; and, as soon as I heard his voice and looked in his face, I was mollified, and against my will, as it were, obliged to listen to him.

' "Ah, madam," he sighed, "such is the change that often comes over the affairs of men! There was a time when ladies boasted of having been robbed by Barrington. Many whom I had never robbed gave it out that I had done so, simply that they might be talked about. Alas! such is the weakness of poor human nature that some people care not by what means they associate their names with the name of any celebrity. I was in power then, not in bondage. 'Barrington has my diamond ear-rings!' once exclaimed the old Countess of Kettlebank, clasping her hands. Her ladyship's statement was not true. Her diamonds were paste, and she knew it, and I caused them to be returned to her. Had you not a pair of very small pearl-drops in your ears this morning, madam?"

'I placed my hands to my ears, and discovered that the drops were gone. Again my anger returned, and I said, "How dared you, sir, place your fingers on my face?"

' "Upon my sacred word and honour, madam," he replied, placing his hand over his left breast, and bowing, "I did nothing of the kind! The ear is the most sensitive part of the human body to the touch of another person. Had I touched your ear my hope of having these drops in my waistcoat pocket would have been gone. It was the springs only that I touched, and the drops fell into the palm of my left hand." He placed the ear-rings on the table, and made me another very low bow.

' "And when did you deprive me of them?" I asked him.

' "When I was discoursing on floriculture, you had occasion several times to incline your head towards your charming children, and gently reprove them for interrupting me. It was on one of these occasions that the deed was quickly done. The dear children were the unconscious confederates in my crime—if crime you still consider it—since I have told you, and I spoke the truth; that it was not for the sake of gain, but simply to satisfy a passionate curiosity. It was as delicate and as difficult an operation as any I ever performed in the whole course of my professional career."

'There was a peculiar quaintness of humour and of action thrown into this speech; I could not refrain from laughing. But, to my great satisfaction, the illustrious pickpocket did not join in the laugh. He regarded me with a look of extreme humility, and maintained a respectful silence, which was shortly broken by a loud knocking at the outer door. It was the major, who, suddenly remembering his appointment with Barrington, had contrived to make his escape from Government House, in order to keep it. The major seemed rather surprised to find Barrington in my drawing-room; but he was in such a hurry, and so anxious, that he said nothing on the subject.

'I withdrew to the passage, whence I could overhear all that took place.

' "Now, look here, Barrington," said my husband, impetuously, "I will have no more nonsense. As for a free pardon, or even a conditional pardon, at present, it is out of the question. In getting you a ticket-of-leave, I have done all that I possibly can; and as I am a living man, I give you fair warning that if you do not keep faith with me, I will undo what I have already done. A free pardon! What! Let you loose upon the society of England again? The Colonial Secretary would scout the idea, and severely censure the Governor for recommending such a thing. You know, as well as I do, that if you returned to England to-morrow, and had an income of five thousand a year, you would never be able to keep those fingers of yours quiet."

' "Well, I think you are right, major," said the illustrious personage.

' "Then you will write a letter at once?"

' "I will. But on one condition."

' "Another condition?"

' "Yes."

' "Well, what is that condition? You have so many conditions that I begin to think the necklace will not be forthcoming after all. And, if it be not, by ———."

' "Do not excite yourself to anger, major. I give you my honour——."

' "Your honour! Nonsense! What I want is, the jewel restored to its owner."

' "And it shall be, on condition that you will not be offended, grievously offended, with me for what I have done this day!"

' "What is that?"

' "Summon your good lady, and let her bear witness both for and against me."

'My husband opened the drawing-room door, and called out, "Bessie!"

'As soon as I had made my appearance, Barrington stated the case—all that had transpired—with minute accuracy; nay, more, he acted the entire scene in such a way that it became a little comedy in itself; the characters being himself, myself, and the children, all of which characters he represented with such humour that my husband and myself were several times in fits of laughter. Barrington, however, did not even smile. He affected to regard the little drama (and this made it the more amusing) as a very serious business.

'This play over, my husband again put to Barrington the question, "Will you write that letter for me?"

' "Yes," he replied, "I will; for I see that I am forgiven the liberty I was tempted to take." And seating himself at the table he wrote:

' "Mr Barrington presents his compliments to Mr ———, and requests that a sealed packet, marked DN. No. 27, be immediately delivered to the bearer of this note. In the event of this request not being complied with, Mr Barrington will have an opportunity ere long of explaining to Mr ———, in Sydney, New South Wales, that he (Mr ———) has been guilty of an act of egregious folly."

'Fourteen months passed away, when, one morning, my husband received a letter from a gentleman in the Colonial Office. He clapped his hands, cried "Bravo!" and then read as follows:

' "My Dear Major —The great pickpocket has been as good as his word. My lady is again in possession of her brilliants. Do whatever you can for Barrington in the Colony; but keep a sharp eye upon him, lest he should come back and once more get hold of that necklace."

'My husband sent for Barrington to inform him of the result of his letter, and he took an opportunity of asking the illustrious man if there were any other valuables which he would like to restore to original owners.

' "Thank you——no!" was the reply. "There are, it is true, sundry little articles in safe custody at home; but, as it is impossible to say what may be in the future, they had better for the present stand in my own name." '

JOHN LANG

Sir Henry Hayes

From Botany Bay, or True Stories of the Early Days of Australia
(1859).
   *Far-fetched as it may seem, the story of Sir Henry Hayes's importation
of Irish soil is quite true.*

Suggested further reading: J. H. M. Abbott, Out of the Past *(1944).*

'Sir Henry Hayes,' said the old lady one day to me, 'was what
was called in Sydney "a Special". Specials were gentlemen by
birth and education, who had been convicted of offences which,
however heinous in a legal point of view, did not involve any
particular degree of baseness. For instance, Major B., who, in
a violent fit of passion, stabbed his footman for accidentally
spilling some soup and soiling the King's livery, which the major
was then wearing, was a Special; so was the old German baron*
whose history I gave you on another occasion; and so were those
Irish gentlemen who took a prominent part in the rebellion, and
escaped the fate that awaited Mr Emmett—Specials. All those
kinds of criminals, up to the departure of General Macquarie,
and the arrival of Sir Thomas Brisbane, were not treated like
common thieves and receivers of stolen property, but with great
consideration. If they were not emancipated immediately on
their arrival, they were suffered to be at large without the for-
mality of a ticket-of-leave. They were, in short, treated rather
as prisoners of war on their parole than as prisoners of the Crown
in a penal settlement. Grants of land were not given to them
while they were in actual bondage, but they were permitted to
locate themselves on any unoccupied piece of land in the vicinity

*Baron Wald. See *Fisher's Ghost and Other Stories of the Early Days of Aus-
tralia,* p. 94.

of Sydney. The greater number of them were well supplied with funds by their relations in England, Ireland or Scotland, and erected very comfortable, if not particularly handsome, abodes, and laid out gardens and grounds. General Macquarie went a little too far, perhaps. He not only admitted them to his table as soon as they were emancipated, but he elevated some of them to the magisterial bench.

'Sir Henry built a very pretty little cottage on the estate known as Vaucluse, and upon which the house of Mr William Charles Wentworth now stands. There is not a lovelier site in the known world. Beautifully wooded with evergreens, the land covered with every description of heath, which is in bloom nearly all the year round; a lovely bay of semi-circular shape, and forming one of the inlets of the magnificent harbour of Port Jackson, spread out before the lawn, its dark-blue waters laving the milk-white sand, some black rocks in the distance (known as "the Bottle and Glass") standing out sufficiently far to cause the spray to beat continually over them, the north shore plainly visible across the broad expanse of water—travel where you will, the eye will not rest upon any spot more favoured by Nature than that exquisite valley which was called Vaucluse, in consequence of its resemblance in one or two respects to the Vallis Clausus, where Petrarch, in the words of Lord Byron, "with his melodious tears gave himself to fame". To put his crime out of the question, Sir Henry was a man of very great taste, and an Irish gentleman of the old school.'

'What was his crime?' I asked, in my then ignorance of this colonial celebrity.

'He carried off by force and violence a young lady with whom he was passionately in love, and who had several times refused his offers of marriage. The penalty of the offence was transportation for life. I am not quite sure that he was not, in the first instance, sentenced to be hanged. My husband, in common with many officers, was partial to Hayes, who could be very witty and amusing, and who, whatever may have been his habits in early life, led a most temperate and exemplary life in the colony of New South Wales. He was surrounded by every comfort that money could purchase, and was always glad to see persons of whom he was in the habit of speaking as "those of my own order". The only defect in his manner was that his air was too patronizing.

'That Hayes was perfectly mad on the crime that led to his banishment there could not be the slightest question; but upon all other points no one could be more rational. That his statements with reference to his case were untrue, no one who read the report of his trial could doubt for a single moment, but that Hayes himself believed his own version to be the correct one was equally certain. I never saw Sir Henry but twice, and I must do him the justice to say that on neither occasion did he speak of his case. He was by far too well bred to think of making the faintest allusion to it. By the way, he did once say in my presence, on the occasion of his killing a fly with the handle of a carving-fork, "That's how I should like to crush John Philpot Curran"; but upon my husband remarking to him, "My wife never heard of that person, Hayes", Sir Henry made me a very low bow, begged me a million pardons, and instantly changed the theme.'

'Why was he so inveterate with regard to Mr Curran?' I inquired.

'It was Mr Curran, my husband told me, who prosecuted Sir Henry Hayes,' was the old lady's reply. 'I told you that I only saw Sir Henry twice,' she continued. 'On the first occasion he called at our house in a state of great nervous excitement. After being introduced to me, and speaking for a while on various subjects, he thus addressed my husband: "My dear major, for the last eleven days I have suffered agonies of mind, and have been praying, from early dawn to dusky night, almost without intermission, to my favourite saint, Saint Patrick. But he seems to take no more notice of me, nor of my prayers, than if I were some wretched thief in a road-gang, with manacles on my leg, and a stone-breaking hammer in my hand."

' "What is the matter, that you require the aid of Saint Patrick?" said my husband.

' "The matter!" replied Sir Henry. "You are aware, perhaps, that that part of the country where I live literally swarms with snakes, yellow snakes, diamond snakes, carpet snakes—in short, every species of snake in the known world. Now, so long as they confined themselves to the lawn and the garden, I did not so much mind. It was bad enough to have them there, but, with caution, I could avoid them. The brutes, however, have lately taken to invade the house. We have killed them in the verandah, and in every room, including the kitchen. Now, it was in consequence of this that I addressed my prayers to Saint Patrick, and suggested that he might whisper to them to go into other people's houses, and not mine, in order to gratify their curiosity concerning the habits of civilized man; but to no purpose. Last night I found a gentleman, six feet long, and as black as a coal, coiled up on my white counterpane; and another of the same dimensions underneath the bed. However, I am determined they shall not banish me from that abode, but that I will banish them; or, at all events, keep them at a proper distance—say, a distance of at least fifty yards from any part of the house. And what I want you to do, my dear major, is to render me some assistance in the matter."

' "What do you propose doing?" my husband inquired.

' "You know perfectly well, my excellent friend," continued Sir Henry, "that Saint Patrick so managed matters that no snake could ever live on or near Irish soil. The very smell of it is more than enough for them. It will be a matter of time and money; but to carry out my project I am most firmly resolved."

' "What do you propose doing, and how can I aid you?" said the major.

' "Hark ye!" returned Sir Henry. "I intend to import to this country about five hundred tons of genuine Irish bog, which shall be dug from the estate of a friend of mine. It shall come out in large biscuit barrels. I shall then have a trench dug round my premises, six feet wide and two feet deep; and this trench the Irish earth shall fill."

' "And do you really believe that Australian snakes will be kept away by your Irish soil, Sir Henry?" said the major.

' "Believe! Of course, I do. I am quite certain of it," responded Hayes. "This very day I have written to my friend in Ireland, and told him to employ an agent to carry out my wishes, and have the bog-earth taken down to Cork for shipment. Now, the favour I have to ask of you is this: To write, in your official capacity, a letter to my agent, which I will enclose to him—such a letter as will lead the captains and doctors of the ships that touch at Cork, to fill up the complement of convicts for these shores, to suppose that the soil is for Government, and required for botanical purposes; and further, I want you to allow it to be consigned to yourself or the Colonial Secretary. Each ship might remove a quantity of its stone ballast, and put the casks of bog in its stead. By these means, I would get it all the quicker."

'My husband endeavoured to laugh Sir Henry out of his idea, but in vain. He was firm, and said:

' "If you won't assist me, I must instruct them to charter a ship for the especial purpose, and that would cost a very serious sum of money."

'My husband, of course, could not think of acting in the matter without previously obtaining the consent of the Governor, who was so amused at the superstitious character of Hayes' enterprise, that His Excellency caused the required letter to be written, and handed to him.

'About a year afterwards, the first instalment of the soil arrived—some forty barrels—and was conveyed from Sydney to Vaucluse (a distance of six miles) by water; and within the next year the entire quantity had reached its destination. The trench, in the meantime, had been dug, and all was now ready for "circumventing", as Sir Henry expressed it, "the premises and the vipers at one blow."

'My husband and myself and a large party of ladies and gentlemen went down to Vaucluse in the Government barges to witness the operation of filling in the trench. The superintendent of convicts—a countryman of Hayes, and who believed as implicitly as Hayes himself did in the virtue of Irish soil with regard to vipers—lent Sir Henry barrows and shovels and a gang consisting of seventy-five men—all of them Irishmen—in order to complete the work as rapidly as possible. Sir Henry, in person, superintended, and was alternately pathetic and jocular. Some of his running commentaries on Saint Patrick and his wonderful powers, and some snatches of song that he sang in honour of the saint, convulsed with laughter all those who stood around him. The work over, one or two of the men asked for a small quantity of the sacred earth, and Sir Henry said:

' "Well, take it and welcome; but I would rather have given you its weight in gold."

'Strange to say, from that time forward, Sir Henry Hayes was not visited by snakes. They did not vacate the grounds in the vicinity of Vaucluse, but none were ever seen within the magic circle formed of Irish earth. Whether the charm is worn out, and whether the Wentworths are invaded as was Sir Henry, I know not. But this I know, that Captain Piper, who held the appointment of naval officer in the colony, to whom Vaucluse was subsequently granted, and from whom Mr Wentworth purchased it, assured me that, during many years he lived there with his family, no venomous reptile had ever been killed or observed within Hayes' enclosure, notwithstanding they were plentiful enough beyond it.'

I wish the reader to understand that I have simply related the above story as it was told to me, and that I do not offer any opinion as to the efficacy or otherwise of Irish soil in keeping away Australian snakes from any spot upon which it may be placed.

After a pause, the old lady resumed:

'I ought to have mentioned that it was on the seventeenth of March, Saint Patrick's day, that this curious ceremony was performed, and that at its conclusion, at half-past four in the afternoon, we dined with Sir Henry in a large tent formed of the old sails of a ship, which were lent to him for the occasion by the captain of the vessel then lying in the harbour. Sir Henry was in excellent spirits, and, when the evening closed in he sang several Irish melodies with great sweetness and pathos. To every one present he made himself extremely agreeable, and, on the whole, I never spent a happier day in my life albeit I was the guest of a Special convict.'

JOHN LANG

Kate Crawford

From Botany Bay, or True Stories of the Early Days of Australia *(1859).*

The events of this story are based on historical fact; and Kate Crawford's fall and rise are similar in many respects to those of Mary Haydock (1777–1855) who, at thirteen years of age, was convicted of stealing a horse, was transported to New South Wales (arriving at Sydney in 1792), married Thomas Reibey, a shipping officer, and eventually became one of the richest women in the colony.

Suggested further reading: Kathleen J. Pullen, Mary Reibey *(1975).*

'We had several female Specials,' said the old lady; 'but the most remarkable of them was Kate Crawford, Beautiful Kitty, as she used to be called. She was very handsome, certainly, and not more than nineteen when she arrived in the colony.'

'What had been her condition in life?' I asked.

'She was the daughter of a Yorkshire squire. In short, she was a lady by birth,' was the reply, 'and had received the education of persons in her father's position and circumstances, and she was accomplished, according to the standard of that day.'

'And what was her crime?'

'Horse-stealing.'

'Horse-stealing!'

'Yes. That was the offence of which she was convicted, and, in those barbaric days, sentenced to be hanged. That sentence, however, was commuted to transportation for fourteen years.'

'Rather a strange offence for a young lady to commit,' I remarked.

'Very true; but you must hear the particulars, just as she related them to me, and to several other ladies who took a very great interest in her. And remember, that all she told us—I mean all the facts she stated—corresponded exactly with those detailed in the report of her trial, which was subsequently, at her request, obtained from England. In one sense of the word, Kate was a very bold girl; in another sense, she was the very reverse of bold. Her manners were in perfect harmony with her person—soft, gentle and feminine; but, if she were resolved upon carrying out any project, great indeed must have been the obstacle she would not surmount. Her story, as she told it, was this:

' "My father, Squire Crawford, and one Squire Pack, lived within a mile of each other. Their estates adjoined. Squire Pack had a son, John Pack, of about twenty-four years of age. I was then between seventeen and eighteen. John Pack was an only son, and I was an only daughter. Both Squire Pack and my father were widowers, and had housekeepers. The old people, over their bowls of punch one night, settled that John Pack should be my husband. Now, it so happened that John Pack—whom I liked very much, he was such a good-natured goosey—was already in love, and secretly engaged to a farmer's daughter, a stout, tall, red-haired girl with blue eyes and a very florid, but clear, complexion. Just the girl in short, to captivate poor John whose taste was not particularly refined. She had, besides, the exact amount of learning to suit poor John, who was not an erudite person by any means. I, too, had a secret engagement with a younger son of Sir Francis Bowman, and who was a lieutenant in a regiment of foot. Squire Pack and my father were both great tyrants, and to have offered the slightest opposition to their plans would possibly have led to their putting into execution, respectively, that threat which was constantly on the lips of either of them: I'll turn you out of doors, and cut you off with a shilling! John Pack and I, therefore, came to an understanding. We were to be lovers in the presence of the old people; but to every other intent and purpose, we were to assist each other in corresponding with our true loves—trusting, as we did, to some accident or some quarrel between our fathers to annul the marriage contract they had entered into on our behalf. Matters went on this way for several months, and nothing could be more satisfactory to us young people. John Pack frequently carried letters and messages for me, and I as frequently did the same for him. Squire Pack and my father used to quarrel once in every year, and for a month or two were the most implacable enemies; but, at the end of such term, the one or the other would give way, make an advance (which was always met), shake hands, and become as good friends as ever. The truth was, that when the evenings drew in, they missed their game of cribbage; for John Pack was a very sleepy person over cards, and, as for myself, I could never play at any game except beggar-my-neighbour.

' "One morning in the month of December the hounds met a few miles from our house. Squire Pack and my father rode to cover together. John Pack, who had brought me a letter from my lover, accompanied them, and joined the meet. The moment they were out of the gate, I broke the seal, and read as follows:

' "Dearest Kate,—If you possibly can, meet me on the Halifax road, near the Hen and Chickens. I will be there at eleven, and will wait till two in the hope of seeing you. I have something very important to communicate. My father intends having an interview with your father the day after to-morrow. I would have ridden over to the Hatch, only you gave me such good reasons for not doing so, or even coming near the place at present. In haste.

Ever affectionately yours,
GEORGE BOWMAN.

' "The Hen and Chickens, a roadside inn, was distant from the Hatch (the name of my father's house) about six miles; and, when I received my lover's letter, it was nearly half-past ten o'clock. I flew to the stables, and ordered the groom to saddle my horse. To my disgust, he informed me that the animal was as lame as a cat. I then ordered him to put my saddle on Marlborough, a second hunter of my father's. The groom told me that the horse had been taken to a point called Milebush, where the squire expected to pick him up fresh. I then said, 'Saddle the old mare,' and was given to understand that she had gone to the farrier's to be shod. What was to be done? I deliberated for a few minutes, and then ordered the groom to take my side-saddle and bridle, and follow me to Squire Pack's, and hastily attiring myself in my riding-habit and hat, I ran across the fields as fast as I could, and made for the stables of our neighbour. The only saddle-horse in the squire's stables at the time was a magnificent thoroughbred colt, which had just been broken in; and this colt the squire's groom was not disposed to saddle for me without the squire's personal order. Becoming very impatient, for it then wanted only three minutes to eleven, I shook my whip at the groom, and said: 'Saddle him this instant. Refuse at your peril! You shall be discharged this very night!' All Squire Pack's servants, as well as our own, believed that I was to be John Pack's wife, and the groom, fearful of that gentleman's wrath, no longer hesitated to obey my instructions. The colt was saddled and brought out. I mounted him, and laid him along the road at the very top of his speed, perfectly satisfied that John Pack would take care that my father never heard of my adventure, and that his father would say nothing about it—determined, as I was, to have a note for John, to be delivered on his return from the chase.

' "It was exactly nineteen minutes past eleven when I arrived at the Hen and Chickens, and found George Bowman waiting for me. He had walked over from his father's house. The colt I had ridden was so bathed in perspiration that I alighted, and caused him to be taken into a shed and rubbed down. While the stable-boys were so engaged, George and I walked along the road, and discoursed intently on our own affairs for more than an hour and a half. We then returned to the inn, and I gave orders for the colt to be saddled. But, alas! the colt was not in the stable wherein he had been placed after he had been rubbed down, nor was a traveller, who was dressed like a gentleman and who had come to the inn to bait his jaded horse shortly after my arrival, to be found on the premises, though his horse was in one of the stalls—a horse that must have been a very swift and valuable creature in his day, but then rather old and broken-winded. There could be no doubt that this person, whoever he might be, had made the exchange, and ridden away unseen while the stable-boys were taking their dinner. A well-dressed man had ridden swiftly past George and myself whilst we were walking on the road; but we were far too much engrossed in conversation to take any particular notice of himself or the steed he was riding. Under these awkward and distressing circumstances, I scarcely knew what to do. It was now past two o'clock, and I was anxious to return to my home. I therefore (accompanied by George Bowman to the very edge of our grounds), proceeded on foot. As soon as I was in my own room, I divested myself of my riding-habit, and wrote a letter to John Pack, requesting him to see me at the

earliest moment possible. It was past four o'clock when my
father returned, and the moment I saw him I discovered that he
was much the worse for the refreshment he had taken while
absent from home. He told me, and it was quite true, that Jack
Pack had had a bad fall in the field, had broken his thigh and
smashed his head, and that he was then lying in a dangerous state
at a public-house not far from Bradford. I begged of him to let
me go and see the sufferer. But he said No! and then informed
me that he had had such a violent quarrel with Squire Pack, that
they could never be on speaking terms again. It was all about
the settlements, he said; that the old thief wanted to hold off
coming down with any money till his death; that he (Squire
Pack) had broken his word; that he (my father) had given him
a good bellyful of his mind; that he told the squire that neither
he nor his father before him were born in wedlock; and that, after
all, it would be a disgrace for a Crawford to have a Pack for a
husband. All this distressed me very much; but I still hoped that
this, like their other quarrels, would be made up ere long, and
that, in the meantime, poor John Pack would recover, and Sir
Francis Bowman tempt my father to listen to the liberal pro-
posals he was about to make to him with respect to my union
with George. It was, however, a frightfully anxious night that
I passed. My sleep, when it at last stole over me, was a troubled
one, and my dreams a succession of horror upon horror. When
I awoke, I fancied that all was a dream—the accident to John
Pack, the quarrel between my father and the squire, the meeting
between myself and George Bowman, and the loss of the colt
at the Hen and Chickens. But, alas! I was speedily awakened to
the reality of my father calling out 'Kate! Kate! Come here!
What have you been about? Here are the officers of justice come
to take you before the magistrate!' I ran down stairs, confessed
everything, and entreated him to forgive me. Like most of the
old squires, he was a very violent and headstrong man, and on
this occasion his anger was terrific. 'Take her!' he cried to the
officers. 'Take her away! Let her be hanged, for all I care! She
deserves it for deceiving me!'

' "It seems that as soon as Squire Pack heard of my taking the
colt away, he vowed that he would have me tried for horse-
stealing, and thus would he disgrace the man who had called him
such vile names and said such bitter things to him. And, in fulfil-

ment of this vow, he went to the nearest magistrate, accompanied by his groom and another servant, and made a deposition upon oath. The magistrate was an old clergyman, to whom Squire Pack had given the 'living', and who was in the habit of responding the words 'of course', to every sentence the squire uttered. A warrant for my apprehension was immediately issued, and I was taken into custody. What happened before the clerical magistrate I cannot recollect; but I can remember being asked several times, 'What has become of the colt?' and replying, 'I don't know'. The consequence was, I was committed to take my trial at the forthcoming assizes, and was meanwhile sent to prison.

' "Whilst I was in those cold and dismal cells, my father never came near me, nor did he write to me, or even send me a message. The only person whom I saw — and that was in the presence of the jailer — was George Bowman, who did all in his power to console me, although, poor boy, his face and shrunken form plainly betrayed that he was bordering on insanity caused by grief. George told me that Sir Francis Bowman had spoken to Squire Pack; but the squire would not listen to him, and that he had declined to receive the value, or double the value, of the colt which had been 'stolen' by me—swearing that 'the law should take its course'.

' "The day of trial came, and I was arraigned. George Bowman had retained an able lawyer to defend me, but his advocacy was of no avail. He urged that I had not taken the colt with the intention of stealing it, but of returning it after I had ridden it. To this the other counsel replied, 'Why didn't she return it?' 'Because it was stolen from her at the inn,' was the rejoinder. This the jury regarded as a very fond [foolish] tale, and found me guilty; whereupon the judge put on the black cap, and sentenced me to be hanged by the neck until I was dead!

' "What happened afterwards, whom I saw, or what they said I know not. I was in a perfect lethargy, and did not recover my senses until more than half of the voyage to the colony was completed." '

Here the old lady paused for a brief while, and then resumed.

'What Kate's sufferings must have been, when she was conscious of what was passing around her, it would, indeed, be difficult to describe. She had not only to bear the companionship of the three hundred degraded wretches who were her fellow-passengers, but to withstand the unseemly attentions of the Navy surgeon, who had charge of the convicts, and who had become enamoured of her extreme beauty. The captain of the vessel, also, fell desperately in love with her, and on several occasions proposed to marry her, abandon the sea, and settle in the colony. The surgeon having heard of this, quarrelled with the captain, and threatened Kate that if she ever spoke or listened to the captain again, he would have her hair cut off, and that she should be publicly flogged. (He had the power, you know, of inflicting such punishment upon any female convict who incurred his displeasure.) The captain being informed by one of his officers of this threat, thrashed the surgeon on the quarter-deck, to the delight of the women, who looked on and cried "Bravo!" The surgeon called the guard—fifty soldiers (recruits). But as each man had his sweetheart on board, and as the cause was regarded as the "women's cause", the guard declined to interfere in the matter. This was a sad state of affairs, no doubt, so far as discipline was concerned; but it tended very materially to Kate Crawford's advantage. Amidst the strife and contending passions of the two men, she was safe in that sense of the word most desirable to herself. When the ship arrived in the harbour, the surgeon preferred a complaint against the captain and his officers. There was an investigation, which resulted in a manner rather prejudicial to the surgeon, and the Governor gave an order that he was not to be permitted to depart the colony until the pleasure of his Majesty's Government was known. Such pleasure was known about a year afterwards. It was to the effect that the surgeon was to be sent to England, under an arrest, in the first man-of-war that touched at Port Jackson. He had made several statements and admissions at the investigation to warrant and insure his dismissal from the service of the State.

'Soon after her arrival, Kate had to undergo fresh persecutions. She was "applied for" by at least twenty unmarried officers, each of whom was anxious to have her "assigned" to him as a servant. It was not uncommon in those days for officers to marry their assigned servants, and make them sell rum at the back doors of their private houses, or quarters, to private soldiers and convicts at a dump (fifteen pence) a glass. It was by these means that many of them amassed large wealth in ready money.'

'Did the Government know of this?' I asked.

'That is a question I decline to answer,' replied the old lady. 'But this I know, that when the duty was taken off rum imported to the colony, very few people were licensed to keep public-houses. However, none of these gentlemen were destined to be the master of Kate Crawford. The statement she made at the investigation aroused the sympathy of Mrs Macquarie (the Governor's wife), who enlisted the respect and affection of all who knew her. Mrs Macquarie was driven in her private carriage to the factory at Parramatta—an institution to which all unassigned convicts were taken on their arrival in Sydney—and had an interview with the unfortunate girl. I accompanied Mrs Macquarie on that occasion.

'When Kate was brought by the matron-superintendent into the little room in which Mrs Macquarie and myself were seated, she was dressed in the uniform garb of females under sentence of transportation: the commonest calico print gown, a white apron, white cap without frills or strings, thickly-soled shoes, and no stockings. The dresses were made short, so that the ankles and the lower part of the legs were visible, while the arms were perfectly bare from the elbow-joint. Nevertheless, in those hideous garments, Kate still preserved the bearing of a well-bred gentlewoman. There was no low curtsey, no "may it please your ladyship", no folding of the hands; but there was a gentle inclination of the head and of the body, and an honest, modest look, which would at once have satisfied the most suspicious person in the world that the girl was incapable of committing any crime. And when Mrs Macquarie, with a graceful movement of the hand, requested her to be seated, she thanked and obliged the old lady, simultaneously.

' "I have not come to see you out of mere curiosity," said Mrs Macquarie, "nor have I come to gloat over the sight of a young lady in such a position as that in which you are now placed. I simply came, armed with the authority of the Governor, to know by what means your sojourn in this colony may be rendered the least painful."

'On hearing these words of unexpected kindness, the poor girl burst into passionate tears, and Mrs Macquarie and myself followed her example.

'When she was calmed, and in a condition to listen, Mrs Macquarie again put the question to her, and the poor girl replied, in broken accents, "Do with me, or for me, whatever your kind heart may dictate."

' "Then you shall live," said Mrs Macquarie, "in private apartments, in the house of Mr Kherwin, the chief constable of Parramatta, whose wife shall make you as comfortable as circumstances will admit of. Under that roof you will be perfectly safe, and protected from every species of annoyance. And if you will allow me, I will send you the means of providing yourself with more suitable apparel than that you are now wearing."

'Poor Kate expressed her gratitude in becoming terms, and we took our departure. Mrs Macquarie then ordered the coachman to drive to the house of the chief constable, and expressed to that functionary her wishes, which were tantamount to orders; and that very night Kate Crawford occupied a room in the small but cleanly cottage of the Kherwins. They were very respectable people, the Kherwins; and Mrs Macquarie arranged that Kate was to board with them. I don't know whether Kherwin and his wife were recompensed by a payment of money or a grant of land, but I am satisfied that they lost nothing by the attentions they showed to their unhappy charge.

'Whenever the major and myself went to Parramatta we never failed to pay Kate a visit, and have a long chat with her. On one occasion she told us that she had received a reply to a letter she had written to a friend in England. Her old lover, George Bowman, she said, had, shortly after her conviction, become insane, and was a hopeless lunatic in an asylum. Her father had married a young damsel, and had by her an infant son. John Pack, when he recovered, and came to know the cruel course of conduct his father had pursued, quarrelled with the old man, flogged him in his passion, and then married Peggy, and became a farmer on his own account. Squire Pack, too, had married a young maiden, and had made up his quarrel with Squire Crawford.

Kate was only three years a prisoner of the Crown, or (to speak in the coarser phrase) a convict. General Macquarie, one morning, accompanied by Mrs Macquarie, all the chief officials, and their wives, journeyed to Parramatta. The cortege drew up opposite to the chief constable's cottage. The general and Mrs

Macquarie were the only persons who alighted. After a brief absence they returned, bringing with them poor Kate Crawford, whom the general handed into his carriage, and then ordered the postillion to go to Government House. (There is a Government House in Parramatta.) There, in the presence of all assembled, the dear old general presented Kate with the King's pardon, and at the same time handed to her a piece of parchment, sealed with the seal of the colony, and bearing the general's own signature. It was the title-deed of a grant of land, of two thousand acres, within forty miles of Sydney, and situated in one of the best and most alluvial districts. This ceremony over, the old general led her to the dining-room, where luncheon was ready. The poor girl—she was then only twenty-three—was evidently much overcome by her feelings; but she struggled hard to subdue them, and succeeded.'

'And what became of her?' I asked.

'You shall hear,' said the old lady. 'While she was under the protection of the chief constable, Kate was not idle. She assisted Mrs Kherwin in all matters connected with the household. The cows, the pigs, the poultry, etc., had each and all some share of her attention. And she kept the accounts—for the Kherwins sold the product of the animals which they reared. In short, although she did not cease to be what the vulgar call a "fine lady", she made herself a woman of business, and a shrewd one, too—not that she ever took advantage of those with whom she dealt.

'Now free to do what she pleased, and with a grant of land in her possession, Kate resolved upon remaining in the colony, and devoted herself to farming and the rearing of cattle. Both the general and Mrs Macquarie were so fond of her, that any favour she asked was at once accorded. She applied for fifteen convicts; they were assigned to her. She then engaged a very respectable overseer—a man of firmness and integrity. She borrowed £300, wherewith to commence operations, and build a house. At the end of two years she paid off this debt, and had a considerable balance in hand. The wheat and the Indian maize grown upon her farm always brought the highest price in the market, and she was equally fortunate with her livestock. Many offers of marriage were made to her, year after year, by persons in eligible positions and circumstances; but Mrs Crawford, as she now called herself, had determined on remaining single. She had built for herself a vehicle called a sulky, a gig which had a seat for the accommodation of one person only, and in this she used to drive to Sydney once in every year. Upon all these occasions she was a guest at Government House. In 1823, she was the owner of £12,000 in money, which was invested on mortgage of landed property in the town of Sydney; and in 1837, when I last saw her and laughingly said, "You must be frightfully rich by this time, Kitty?" she replied, "Well, if I were to die now, there would be almost £120,000 to be divided amongst those who are mentioned in my will. Your boys are down for a few pounds—not that I fancy they will ever want them." '

'Is she still alive?' I asked.

'Yes,' replied the old lady, 'and likely to live for the next twenty years; for although she had many days of sorrow, she never had one of sickness, to my knowledge.'

Since the history of Mrs Crawford was related to me, she has departed this life. On asking the gentleman who gave me this story what she died possessed of, he answered, 'The value of her estate, real and personal, was as nearly as possible half a million sterling.'

ANONYMOUS

The Bloody Field of Wheogo

This scathing ballad, reprinted from an 1862 issue of the Sydney Morning Herald *by Frank Clune in his* Wild Colonial Boys *(1948), refers to an incident in the career of the bushranger Frank Gardiner during the year 1862. Sir Frederick Pottinger, Inspector of Police in the Forbes district of New South Wales at that time, was notoriously inefficient in his attempts to capture the leading members of the Gardiner–Ben Hall gang of outlaws, who ranged boldly through the Lachlan River territory in the early 1860s. The incident referred to in this ballad concerned Gardiner's visit to his mistress, Kitty Brown, and Pottinger's abortive efforts to capture him. Pottinger, having missed his chance to arrest Gardiner, took a lad of seventeen, young John Walsh, and charged him with being an accomplice of the bushranger.*

The moon rides high in a starry sky,
And, through the midnight gloom,
A faery scene of woodland green
Her silver rays illume.

Dark mountains show a ridge of snow
Against the deep blue sky,
And a winding stream with sparkling gleam
Flows merrily murmuring by.

Not a sound is heard, save a bough when stirred
By the night-wind's moaning sigh,
Or, piercing and shrill, echoed by the hill,
A curlew's mournful cry.

And twinkling bright in the shadowy night
A lonely taper shines,

And seated there is a wanton fair
Who in amorous sadness pines.

For her lord is gone, and she sits alone,
Alone in her mountain home!
But 'twas not her lord that she deplored,
For she liked to see him roam.

The joy of her heart is a bushranger smart
Who, lion-like, prowls in the night;
And with supper all spread, and a four-post bed,
She waits by the flickering light.

Equipped for fight, in trappings bright,
Came a band of warriors there,
By gallant Sir Fred right gallantly led,
The 'ranger to seize in a snare.

They spread all around, and the house they surround,
Nine men with revolver and gun;
'A reward's on his head!' cried the gallant Sir Fred,
'And we're nine to the bushranger's one!'

Still gleamed the light in the shades of the night,
And still the pale moon shone;
But no 'ranger came to cheer the dame
As she sat by the window alone.

The warriors bold were freezing with cold,
And wished they were in their beds,
When the echoing beat of a horse's feet
Sent the blood in a rush to their heads!

At gentle speed on snow-white steed
And singing a joyous song
To the beckoning light in the shadowy night
The bushranger rides along.

A stalwart man was he to scan,
And flushed with ruffian pride;

In many a fray he had won the day
And the 'New Police' defied.

Up started then Sir Fred and his men
With cocked carbines in hand
And called aloud to the 'ranger proud
On pain of death to 'stand'.

But the 'ranger proud, he laughed aloud,
And bounding rode away,
While Sir Frederick Pott shut his eyes for a shot
And missed—in his usual way.

His troopers then like valiant men,
With their carbines blazed away.
The whistling lead on its mission sped,
But whither, none can say.

The snow-white steed at gentle speed
Bore the 'ranger from their view
And left Sir Fred to return to bed—
There was nothing else to do.

But Sir Frederick Pott with rage was hot
As he looked at his warriors eight.
They were nine to one, with revolver and gun!
He cursed his luckless fate.

He shuddered to think how his glory would sink
When the country heard of the mess
And the tale was told of his exploit bold
In the columns of the Press.

In fury then he marched his men
To the home of the wanton fair;
With warlike din they entered in
To search and ransack there.

In slumber sound a boy they found,
And brave Sir Frederick said:

'By a flash in the pan we missed the man,
So we'll take the boy instead!'

ANONYMOUS

A West Country Ballad

An ironical ballad of the year 1863, reprinted from the Sydney Empire
by Frank Clune in his Wild Colonial Boys *(1948). It refers to an attempt
by Sub-Inspector Norton of the Forbes (NSW) police to capture the bushranger Frank Gardiner, an attempt that led to Norton's own ignominious
hold-up and disarming by the outlaw. In actual fact it was Ben Hall who
was the bushranger involved in this episode; but the ballad-maker didn't
know this at the time. The 'Black Billee' referred to was Billy Dargin,
a police blacktracker.*

───────

This is the tale of Norton
Who vowed a vow, by zounds,
To catch the varlet Gardiner
And win a thousand pounds.

'Come hither, come hither, my little page,
Whom men call Black Billee,
And saddle me up my jolly brown steed
And bring my pistols three.

'A plan have I within my head,
By which I will surround
The rascal Gardiner and his gang,
And win a thousand pound!'

Then up he rose, that little black boy,
And grinned his broad grins three:
'You bin catch that fella Gardiner,
You budgeree Peeler be.'

Then Norton mounted his jolly brown steed,
And himself was hung about

With chains and ropes and handicuffs,
To catch the rabble rout.

He looked so fierce, when he sallied forth
All booted, spurred, and saddled,
That all the little dogs tucked in their tails
And quickly off skedaddled.

On top of the Weddin Mountains stood
Bold General Gardiner,
In cabbage-tree hat and scarlet shirt
And all devoid of fear.

'What dost thou here, in my domain
In suchlike warlike gear?'
Then answered Norton: 'It's you I seek,
Bold Francis Gardiner.

'Of course thou wilt my prisoner be,
Both thou and all thy force,
And quietly come along with me!'
Grinned Gardiner: 'Oh, of course!'

'But tarry a while, Inspector, Sir,
Become a guest of mine,
Go not so soon 'til well-nigh noon,
I prithee stay and dine.

'And thou shalt taste our bushland fare
Of lobster and sardine,
Washed down with many a noggin
Of good Old Tom and gin.

'Give me thy pistols and thy sword,
I'll also take thy watch
To see what was the time of day
When thou did'st Gardiner catch!'

Then Gardiner loudly laughed Ho! Ho!
His merry men laughed He! He!

But Norton laughed a faint Ha! Ha!
The joke he could not see.

Quoth Gardiner: 'Please don't leave us yet,
Thy company is so good.
Thou surely would'st not go—besides
Thou could'st not if thou would.

'Thy solemn word we now must have
That arms thou wilt not bear
'Gainst me, or 'gainst my merry men all—
Then back thou may'st repair.'

So his parole he then did give,
Bold Norton brave and true,
That arms he ne'er again would bear
'Gainst Gardiner and his crew.

Then rode he home, as the story goes,
Although some people say
It is a tale for the marines,
And he dreamt it as he lay.

And naughty people wink their eyes
And say with many a grin:
'It must have been the lobsters,
Washed down with too much gin!'

CHARLES THATCHER

The Lady and the Bullock Driver

Thatcher, the self-styled 'Colonial Minstrel', composed and sang songs on contemporary themes to audiences of gold-diggers at Bendigo (Victoria) and elsewhere during the 1850s and early 1860s. 'The Lady and the Bullock Driver A Real Fact!!!', based on the well-known propensity of teamsters to give open vent to their frustrations in volleys of profane language, was included in Thatcher's Colonial Minstrel *(1864).*

A new original song written and sung by Thatcher with immense applause.

Air: Drops of Brandy

> A squatter who lived Bathurst way,
>   And owned a magnificent station,
> Rode down to Sydney one day,
>   In the course of his peregrination;
> He stuck up to a young lady there,
>   Her beauty was highly delectable,
> Her complexion was lovely and fair,
>   And her family very respectable.
>
> Her parients gave their consent,
>   And determined no longer to tarry,
> To the Church of Saint James's they went,
>   And this handsome young girl he did marry;
> In Sydney they cut a great dash,
>   For often they'd both go out driving,
> And as he had plenty of cash,
>   To please her he always was striving.

His overseer kept writing down,
   And begged that he'd soon be returning,
And as he'd been some time in town,
   For the bush once again he was yearning;
So says he, 'You can ride in the dray,
   If you're not too proud, Mrs Potter';
'Why should I be proud?' she did say,
   'For ain't I the wife of a squatter?'

Bullock drivers of course you all know,
   Are queer specimens of humanity,
The words from their mouths too that flow,
   Evince a most horrid profanity.
So his master sings out, 'Come here, Dick;'
   Up walks the uncouth bullock driver;
'I'll give you the sack pretty quick,
   If my wife you offend with your guiver.'

Says he, 'Not a bad word you'll speak
   On your journey now up to the station,
And if you get struck in a creek,
   Don't curse, but use gentle persuasion:
I'll give you five pounds, I declare,
   If you use no expressions improper,
But if my wife once hears you swear,
   D——n me, if I give you a copper.'

On the very next day they set out,
   Dick talked to his team with gentility,
The bullocks could not make it out,
   They were stunned by such wond'rous civility;
They stared at poor Dick with surprise,
   To find out what he meant they kept trying,
Not once did he bless 'Nobbler's' eyes,
   Though the whip he was constantly plying.

One day they had very bad luck,
   The bullocks were getting quite lazy,
In a small muddy creek they got stuck,
   And poor Dick went very near crazy;

And loudly at them does he bawl,
   But with it no oaths intersperses,
And of course they would not pull at all,
   For they missed his colonial curses.

And then with a sad troubled brow,
   He tried to appeal to their feelings,
Called each one of them an old cow,
   Whilst blows thick and fast he kept dealing;
The lady began to get cross,
   And looked round in vain for assistance,
And she longed for a nice saddle horse,
   For they still had to go a great distance.

The poor bullock driver looked blue,
   In fact he was almost despairing,
He knew that fair words wouldn't do,
   For bullocks won't move without swearing;
So says he to the lady behind,
   (Alas! his request was unholy)
'I say, mum, will you be so kind
   As to 'low me to damn that 'ere Poley?'

JOHN BOYLE O'REILLY

The Dukite Snake

The Fenian, John Boyle O'Reilly, spent a year (January 1868 to February 1869) in Western Australia as a political prisoner. He escaped to the United States aboard a whaling vessel. He published two works of fiction and a number of poems dealing with Western Australian themes. 'The Dukite Snake' is concerned with an old Australian folk belief. It was reprinted in Douglas Sladen's A Century of Australian Song *(1888). 'Dukite' is now usually spelt 'Dugite'.*

———————

Well, mate, you've asked me about a fellow
You met to-day, in a black-and-yellow
Chain-gang suit, with a pedler's pack,
Or with some such burden, strapped to his back.
Did you meet him square? No, he passed you by?
Well, if you had, and had looked in his eye,
You'd have felt for your irons then and there,
For the light in his eye is a madman's glare.
Ay, mad, poor fellow! I know him well,
And if you're not sleepy just yet, I'll tell
His story—a strange one as ever you heard
Or read; but I'll vouch for it, every word.

You just wait a minute, mate; I must see
How that damper's doing, and make some tea.
You smoke? That's good; for there's plenty of weed
In that wallaby skin. Does your horse feed
In the hobbles? Well, he's got good feed here,
And my own old bush-mare won't interfere.
Done with that meal? Throw it there to the dogs,
And fling on a couple of banksia logs.

And now for the story. That man who goes

Through the bush with the pack and the convict's
   clothes
Has been mad for years; but he does no harm,
And our lonely settlers feel no alarm
When they see or meet him. Poor Dave Sloane
Was a settler once, and a friend of my own.
Some eight years back, in the spring of the year,
Dave came from Scotland and settled here.
A splendid young fellow he was just then,
And one of the bravest and truest men
That I ever met: he was kind as a woman
To all who needed a friend, and no man—
Not even a convict—met with his scorn,
For David Sloane was a gentleman born.
Ay, friend, a gentleman, though it sounds queer,
There's plenty of blue blood flowing out here,
And some younger sons of your 'upper ten'
Can be met with here, first-rate bushmen.
Why, friend, I——
           Bah! curse that dog! you see
This talking so much has affected me.

Well, Sloane came here with an axe and a gun;
He bought four miles of a sandal-wood run.
This bush at that time was a lonesome place;
So lonesome, the sight of a white man's face
Was a blessing, unless it came at night,
And peered in your hut with the cunning fright
Of a runaway convict; and even they
Were welcome, for talk's sake, while they could stay.
Dave lived with me here for a while, and learned
The tricks of the bush—how the snare was laid
In the wallaby track, how traps were made,
How 'possums and kangaroo rats were killed;
And when that was learned, I helped him to build
From mahogany slabs a good bush hut,
And showed him how sandal-wood logs were cut.
I lived up there with him days and days,
For I loved the lad for his honest ways.
I had only one fault to find: at first

Dave worked too hard; for a lad who was nursed,
As he was, in idleness, it was strange
How he cleared that sandal-wood off his range.
From the morning light till the light expired
He was always working, he never tired;
Till at length I began to think his will
Was too much settled on wealth, and still
When I looked at the lad's brown face, and eye
Clear, open, my heart gave such thought the lie.
But one day—for he read my mind—he laid
His hand on my shoulder. 'Don't be afraid,'
Said he, 'that I'm seeking alone for pelf,
I work hard, friend; but 'tis not for myself.'
And he told me then in his quiet tone
Of a girl in Scotland who was his own—
His wife,—'twas for her; 'twas all he could say,
And his clear eye brimmed as he turned away.
After that he told me the simple tale:
They had married for love, and she was to sail
For Australia, when he wrote home and told
The oft-watched-for story of finding gold.

In a year he wrote, and his news was good:
He had bought some cattle and sold his wood.
He said, 'Darling, I've only a hut,——but come.'
Friend, a husband's heart is a true wife's home;
And he knew she'd come. Then he turned his hand
To make neat the house, and prepare the land
For his crops and vines; and made that place
Put on such a smiling and homelike face,
That when she came, and he showed her round
His sandal-wood and his crops in the ground,
And spoke of the future, they cried for joy,
The husband's arm clasping his wife and boy.

Well, friend, if a little of heaven's best bliss
Ever comes from the upper world to this,
It came into that manly bushman's life,
And circled him round with the arms of his wife.
God bless that bright memory! Even to me,

A rough, lonely man, did she seem to be,
While living, an angel of God's pure love,
And now I could pray to her face above.
And David, he loved her as only a man,
With a heart as large as his is, can.
I wondered how they could have lived apart,
For he was her idol, and she his heart.

Friend, there isn't much more of the tale to tell.
I was talking of angels a while since. Well,
Now I'll change to a devil—ay, to a devil!
You needn't start; if a spirit of evil
Ever came to this world its hate to slake
On mankind, it came as a Dukite Snake.

Like? Like the pictures you've seen of sin,
A long red snake—as if what was within
Was fire that gleamed through his glistening skin.
And his eyes—if you could go down to hell,
And come back to your fellows here and tell
What the fire was like, you could find no thing,
Here below on the earth, or up in the sky,
To compare it to but a Dukite's eye!

Now, mark you, these Dukites don't go alone:
There's another near when you see but one;
And beware you of killing that one you see
Without finding the other; for you may be
More than twenty miles from the spot that night,
When camped, but you're tracked by the lone Dukite;
That will follow your trail like Death or Fate,
And kill you as sure as you killed its mate!

Well, poor Dave Sloane had his young wife here
Three months—'Twas just this time of the year;
He had teamed some sandal-wood to the Lasse,
And was homeward bound, when he saw in the grass
A long red snake; he had never been told
Of the Dukite's way,—he jumped to the road
And smashed its flat head with the bullock-goad!

He was proud of the red skin, so he tied
Its tail to the cart, and the snake's blood dyed
The bush on the path he followed that night.

He was early home, and the dead Dukite
Was flung at the door to be skinned next day.
At sunrise next morning he started away
To hunt up his cattle. A three hours' ride
Brought him back; he gazed on his home with pride
And joy in his heart; he jumped from his horse
And entered—to look on his young wife's corse,
And his dead child clutching its mother's clothes
As in fright; and there, as he gazed, arose
From her breast, where 'twas resting, the gleaming
    head
Of the terrible Dukite, as if it said,
'I've had vengeance, my foe; you took all I had.'
And so had the snake—David Sloane was mad!
I rode to his hut just by chance that night,
And there on the threshold the clear moonlight
Showed the two snakes dead. I pushed in the door
With an awful feeling of coming woe:
The dead were stretched on the moonlit floor,
The man held the hand of his wife—his pride,
His poor life's treasure—and crouched by her side.
O God!—I sank with the weight of the blow.
I touched and called him; he heeded me not,
So I dug her grave in a quiet spot,
And lifted them both—her boy on her breast—
And laid them down in the shade to rest.
Then I tried to take my poor friend away,
But he cried so woefully, 'Let me stay
Till she comes again!' that I had no heart
To try to persuade him then to part
From all that was left to him here—her grave;
So I stayed by his side that night, and, save
One heart-cutting cry, he uttered no sound—
O God! that wail—like the wail of a hound!
'Tis six long years since I heard that cry,
But 'twill ring in my ears till the day I die.

Since that fearful night no one has heard
Poor David Sloane utter sound or word.
You have seen to-day how he always goes:
He's been given that suit of convict's clothes
By some prison-officer. On his back
You noticed a load like a pedler's pack?
Well, that's what he lives for; when reason went
Still memory lived, for his days are spent
In searching for Dukites; and year by year
That bundle of skins is growing. 'Tis clear
That the Lord out of evil some good still takes,
For he's clearing the bush of the Dukite snakes.

ANONYMOUS

The Kellys, Byrne and Hart

The sticking-up of a bank at Euroa (Victoria) in late 1878, followed by a daring raid on the town of Jerilderie in southern New South Wales, gave the Kelly gang of bushrangers (Ned and Dan Kelly, Joe Byrne and Steve Hart) all the notoriety they could have wished for. Almost overnight they became fit subjects for hero ballads, of which the following, intended to be sung to the tune of 'The Wearing of the Green', was one of the most popular.
Suggested further reading: Six Authentic Songs of the Kelly Country *(1955); Max Brown,* Australian Son *(1948); Prior and Wannan,* Plundering Sons; A Pictorial History of Australian Bushranging *(1966).*

Oh, Paddy dear, and did you hear
The news that's going round,
On the head of bold Ned Kelly
They have placed two thousand pound.
And on Steve Hart, Joe Byrne and Dan
Two thousand more they'd give,
But if the price was doubled, boys,
The Kelly Gang would live.

'Tis hard to think such plucky hearts
In crime should be employed,
'Tis by police persecution
They have all been much annoyed.
Revenge is sweet, and in the bush
They can defy the law,
Such sticking up and plundering
You never saw before.

'Twas in November, Seventy-eight,
When the Kelly Gang came down,

Just after shooting Kennedy,
To famed Euroa town;
To rob the bank of all its gold
Was their idea that day,
Blood-horses they were mounted on
To make their getaway.

So Kelly marched into the bank,
A cheque all in his hand,
For to have it changed for money
Of Scott he did demand.
And when that he refused him,
He, looking at him straight,
Said, 'See here, my name's Ned Kelly,
And this here man's my mate.'

With pistols pointed at his nut,
Poor Scott did stand amazed,
His stick he would have liked to cut,
But was with funk half crazed;
The poor cashier, with real fear,
Stood trembling at the knees,
But at last they both seen 'twas no use
and handed out the keys.

The safe was quickly gutted then,
The drawers turned out, as well,
The Kellys being quite polite
Like any noble swell.
With flimsies, gold and silver coin,
And threepennies and all
Amounting to two thousand pounds,
They made a glorious haul.

'Now hand out all your firearms,'
The robber boldly said,
'And all your ammunition—
Or a bullet through your head.
Now get your wife and children—
Come, man, now look alive;

All jump into this buggy
And we'll take you for a drive.'

They took them to a station
About three miles away,
And kept them close imprisoned
Until the following day.
The owner of the station
And those in his employ
And a few unwary travellers
Their company did enjoy.

An Indian hawker fell in, too,
As everybody knows,
He came in handy to the gang
By fitting them with clothes.
Then with their worn-out clothing
They made a few bonfires,
And then destroyed the telegraph
By cutting down the wires.

Oh, Paddy dear, do shed a tear,
I can't but sympathize,
Those Kellys are the devils,
For they've made another rise;
This time across the billabong,
On Morgan's ancient beat,
They've robbed the banks of thousands,
And in safety did retreat.

The matter may be serious, Pat,
But still I can't but laugh,
To think the tales the bobbies told
Must all amount to chaff.
They said they had them all hemmed in,
They could not get away,
But they turned up in New South Wales,
And made the journey pay.

They rode into Jerilderie town

At twelve o'clock at night,
Aroused the troopers from their beds,
And gave them an awful fright.
They took them in their night-shirts,
Ashamed I am to tell,
They covered them with revolvers
And locked them in a cell.

They next acquainted the womenfolk
That they were going to stay
And take possession of the camp
Until the following day.
They fed their horses in the stalls
Without the slightest fear,
Then went to rest their weary limbs
Till daylight did appear.

Next morning being Sunday morn
Of course they must be good,
They dressed themselves in troopers' clothes,
And Ned, he chopped some wood.
No one there suspected them,
As troopers they did pass,
And Dan, the most religious one,
Took the sergeant's wife to mass.

They spent the day most pleasantly,
Had plenty of good cheer,
Fried beefsteak and onions,
Tomato-sauce and beer;
The ladies in attendance
Indulged in pleasant talk,
And just to ease the trooper's minds,
They took them for a walk.

On Monday morning early,
Still masters of the ground,
They took their horses to the forge
And had them shod all round;
Then back they came and mounted,

Their plans all laid so well,
In company with the troopers
They stuck up the Royal Hotel.

They bailed up all the occupants,
And placed them in a room,
Saying, 'Do as we command you,
Or death will be your doom.'
A Chinese cook, 'No savvy' cried,
Not knowing what to fear,
But they brought him to his senses
With a lift under the ear.

All who now approached the house
Just shared a similar fate,
In hardly any time at all
The number was twenty-eight.
They shouted freely for all hands,
And paid for all they drank,
And two of them remained in charge,
And two went to the bank.

The farce was here repeated
As I've already told,
They bailed up all the banker's clerks
And robbed them of their gold.
The manager could not be found,
And Kelly, in great wrath,
Searched high and low, and luckily
He found him in his bath.

The robbing o'er, they mounted then
To make a quick retreat,
They swept away with all their loot
By Morgan's ancient beat;
And where they've gone I do not know,
If I did I wouldn't tell,
So now, until I hear from them,
I'll bid you all farewell.

JAMES KIRBY

A Snake Yarn

James Kirby, a pioneer of the Minyip district of Victoria, published his reminiscences, Old Times in the Bush of Australia, *in 1896. Kirby had many good tales to tell, including the two tall stories that follow. They are typical of the taproom jests which were going the rounds of the Australian bush in the 1840s; and similar yarns are still being told in outback pubs to this day.*

If there was one bigger liar than another, 'Squeaky Dick', I think, ought to get the cake.

Squeaky stood up, gave his hat a touch on one side, and said—

'Now, lads, I'll give you a snake yarn, and "sen-I-may-live" it is true, for I seen it with my own eyes.'

'All right Squeaky, go ahead,' from the mob.

'Well, I was never bit by a snake, only twicest.'

'That'll do yer, Squeaky.'

'Come, come now, draw it mild.'

'Stick to the truth and shame the devil.'

'S'help me,' says Squeaky, 'you chaps won't believe a man; I'll knock off.'

'Oh no, Squeaky, go ahead old man.'

'Well, as me and my mate were goin' along the track one day, humping our "blueys", what should I see a bit ahead of us but a thunderin' big black snake; he was over twelve feet long, and pretty thick.

'I had a dorg with me I call "Nip". Nip was death on snakes, so I says to him, "catch him, kill him". Well, lads, the dorg starts for the snake, but, my word, that snake could go; and, mind you, Nip could go a bit, too. Just as Nip got pretty close on to him, the snake gives a curious sort of turn, and in a jiffy whips the end of his tail into his "gob" (mouth) and made a hoop of hisself,

and then, my oath, he *did* go. Why, the hoop stood up so high'
(holding his hand about three feet from the ground to indicate
the size of the hoop). 'No dorg couldn't ketch him; the larst we
seen of him he was goin' straight for a brush fence. Nip was
pretty close on him, and we thought he would nab him at this
fence, but no such luck, for the snake hauled off, goes straight
at the fence, and cleared it like a bird.

'Lawks! How funny it did look, to see that big hoop goin' it,
and flyin' the fence in that way.'

'That'll do yer, Squeaky. We don't believe you ever seen any-
think of the sort.'

'I believe it,' says old Nosey, 'for I seed somethink like it myself, but *my* snake, as soon as he put his tail in his "gob", kept
on swallerin' hisself! Yes, lads, he kept on swallerin' and
swallerin' until there was no snake left.'

'Thankee, Nosey; well, I don't know, it may be true, for all
we know.'

'True,' says Nosey, 'true as gospel.'

JAMES KIRBY

A Dog Named 'Bally'

The shepherd holding forth in a tap-room always endeavours to make it appear that he was a better shepherd than any other. He would go on talking a lot of rubbish as to the way he used *his* sheep, and I must not omit his 'dorg'. Dog yarns were always very acceptable in a tap-room.

One fellow could tell a very good yarn about his 'dorg'.

With half a pint of brandy in one hand, and tumbler in the other, his dirty old hat cocked on one side, he began:

'Well now, lads, you can believe me or believe me not, but I had a little dorg at one time what got me a livin'. I called him Bally. Well, one day I sees the cove (master) a comin'. He wor ridin' and wor goin' past my sheep, so I sen's old Bally roun' 'em, just to show the cove that I wasn't far off, and Bally fetches the sheep to me. Well, the cove, he comes to me again in about a week, and pulls up and has a 'pitch' (talk).

'He says to me, says he, "is that dorg o' yourn any good?"

' "Well," says I, "he ain't bad."

' "I'll give you a quid for him," says he.

' "No," says I, "I won't take that, I give five for him"; so then he says, "I seen him do a smart thing when I was riding by one day last week."

' "What was that?" says I.

' "Well," says he, "when I was going past your sheep, I seen your dorg comin' roun' them, and, my word, he was just in time, for old Dick's sheep would have been boxed with yourn only for the dorg. I never seen you at all at the time, and didn't know where the dorg came from."

' "Oh," says I, "it makes no odds where I am, old Bally knows what to do. Well, now you speak of it, I *do* remember seein' a cove ride by the sheep about a week ago, but I never thought it was you, sir." '

(What is meant by getting boxed is to get joined with another flock, and if two flocks get boxed it means a lot of work, for they had to be driven to the home station and hand drafted.)

The race and swing gate were not in vogue then, or even thought of for several years after. The person who invented these ought to have been made independent by the squatters and others who have to do with sheep, but I think he got nothing for it.

It used to knock the sheep about sadly, this hand drafting, for they had to be caught and lifted over a fence, and it was no child's play to work at that all day, especially if they were large wethers.

' "Well," says the cove, "you won't sell the dorg, Bill?"

' "Not likely," says I, "when I give five quid for him." It was five bob I give for him, but I didn't tell the cove that.

' "Well, look here, Bill," says he, "I am goin' to start shearin' next week, and I want you to come in to the home station, and remain there till we finish."

' "All right, sir," says I; so I goes in on the day he said, but I didn't take old Bally; I knowed it wor the dorg and not me he wanted.

'When I gets to the home station, the cove says to me, "Where's the dorg, Bill?"

' "Oh," says I, "I left him at my hut."

' "You'll have to go and fetch him," says he.

' "Well, no sir," says I, "I don't care about my dorg bein' about at shearin' time, because some of the lads might shake him."

'After a while the cove says—

' "It's the dorg I want, Bill, not you."

' "I thought so," says I. "Well," says I, "I can't let my dorg go for nothin'." (I was gettin' fifteen bob a week.) "So," says I, "if you like to give Bally fifteen bob a week, he shall come."

' "All right," says he, "it's a bargain."

'So you see, lads, I was gettin' fifteen bob, and so was Bally.'

'That'll do yer, Billy,' said one of the lads; and 'That'll do you too,' says Billy.

By these remarks the reader will understand that they did not believe Billy.

The Breelong Blacks

Jimmy Governor, half-Aboriginal, half-white, married to a white woman, could not endure the racist taunts hurled at him by white neighbours at Breelong, in the Dubbo district of northern New South Wales, where he lived and worked. His self-control broke on the night of 20 July 1900; he savagely murdered a number of people, and he paid for this outrage with his life at Darlinghurst Jail, Sydney on 18 January 1901.

A contemporary balladist recorded the bloody events while they were still fresh in the public memory. I have not been able to find out who wrote the verses, and the newspaper cutting containing them, which was sent to me many years ago, remains for me unidentified. Perhaps somebody reading this book will enlighten me as to the source and authorship of this long narrative.

The story of Jimmy Governor, his brother Joe, and a companion, Jack Underwood, is now a part of Australian folklore. It has been retold many times in many different ways—the most notable, perhaps, being Thomas Keneally's novel, The Chant of Jimmie Blacksmith *(1972).*

Suggested further reading: Frank Clune, Jimmy Governor *(1959).*

On the banks of the Wallumburrawong,
What's that? A river, they say.
Well no, it's only a creek
That runs into the Castlereagh;
It was there that the Maubys were murdered,
As no doubt you all may know,
By these blacks: Jackie Underwood,
Jimmie Governor, and his brother Joe.

Jimmie Governor was working for Mauby,
He was splitting posts for a fence,
When Mauby found fault with a hundred—
Of course at the darkies' expense.

Said he, they're not up to the agreement
And I won't for one of them pay.
It was then that the darkies consented
In the bush that the hundred shall lay.

Now after condemning their posts
And then refusing to pay,
Nothing must do old Mauby
But to start carting those posts away.
Of course this nettled the darkies,
So Jimmie and Joe went down,
And Mauby, to save further trouble,
Agreed to give them the crown.

Now Mauby he had no right
In touching those posts at all;
No doubt he thought he was cunning
But it stuck in the darkies' gall.
And there is that brazen-faced women—
I'm alluding to Governor's wife—
Who prompted them on the murders.
She ought to be jailed for life.

For the lies and the yarns she told Jimmie
Of things that the Maubys said,
That for living her life with the blacks
Jimmie and she should be dead;
That's how she worked up the row,
A scheme that she planned up some time,
And if ever the truth gets known
[She] coaxed Underwood into the crime.

You might think I'm hard on the woman
And say I'm not treating her fair,
But when Mrs Mauby was dying
She said that the woman was there.
Elsie Clark who escaped with her life
Heard Mrs Governor say:
Look Jimmie, there goes the girls,
As the teacher and Grace ran away.

Now Mauby he had two places
Not quite a mile between
And the family was separated
On the night that the murder was seen.
Old Mauby, Reggie and Clarkie
Slept in the house below;
The mother, the girls and young Percy
Stayed at the other, you know.

This place had once been a station—
That's if my mind is not wrong.
The old homestead lay more to the river;
And the station was called Breelong.
When Mauby took up the station
And started to live on the same,
He altered a great many things
But he never altered the name.

Now Mauby was known for years
To the blacks on the Castlereagh,
For he would always employ a black
If they happened to come this way.
The Governors they knew all this
And his soft soaping ways as well;
So they waited to strike the blow,
And it was a blow when it fell.

Now the night the deed was done
Was a night without any moon,
The weather was rather cold
It being after the month of June.
They went to the lower place
To visit old Mauby first,
Intending to kill him no doubt,
So anxious for blood was their thirst.

They knew that the Maubys had rifles,
They saw Reggie and Clarkie inside.
If old Mauby had been by himself that night
I believe he would have died.

Not daring to face the men,
For they hadn't a white man's heart,
They found themselves in a fix
Being baffled just there for a start.

'Twas there that they altered their plans
And worked quite a different way;
Jimmie called out to old Mauby,
Said he wanted a bundle of hay.
'Come down in the morning,' said Mauby;
'Very good,' said Jimmie, 'all right';
And he reckoned by what he had seen
That Mauby was there for the night.

For they made for the house above,
Still on their murder bent;
To where the women and children slept
Those cowardly rascals went.
Poor Percy was the first to wake,
And he made a rush for the door,
But Underwood dealt him a blow,
Leaving him dead on the floor.

It was then that dear little Hilda
Ran for her life down the track,
But the poor little soul fell a victim
To the blow of the brutal black,
Who mangled her helpless body
As stunned by the blow she lay;
And when he had reckoned her dead
The murderer made away.

The next to swell the number
Was the teacher, Miss Kurtz, and Grace,
Who, holding each other's hands,
Made off at a rapid pace.
They had beaten the blacks,
And were running to spare their life;
And save it no doubt they would have,
But they were seen by Governor's wife.

'Look, Jimmie, there goes the girls,'
Were the words about the victims said.
The criminal ran them down
And with him [   ]* killed them dead.
The teacher was the first to fall,
Jimmie got to her with spite,
While Grace ran down the track
On that fatal Friday night.

She had nothing on her but a gown,
And that was torn from her back
When part of it caught on a rock
And threw her right down on the track.
Now leaving the teacher dead,
This fiend took after Grace
Who was running along through the bush
To get to the lower place.

When Grace slipped and fell
This gave the darkie a show,
And before she could rise from the ground
He had dealt her a heavy blow.
It seems hard to think that this girl
Who escaped so far till then
Should stumble and stagger and fall
Almost in sight of the men.

While the Governors were slaughtering the women,
Young Bertie, that brave little lad,
Slipped out of the bedroom window
And succeeded in reaching his dad.
He was the first to spread the news
Of the terrible deed that night;
I fancy I see him now,
Describing that horrible sight.

Old Mauby jumped out of his bed.
To the scene of the murder he ran

---

*Word indecipherable (Ed.)

With Reggie and Clarkie behind . . .
They brought with them rifle and gun.
The old man ran through the bush,
The boys came round by the creek;
But the Governors got wind of their coming
And cleared through the bush pretty quick.

Poor Percy lie dead at the door,
Mrs Mauby dying close by;
Elsie Clarke out in the garden,
All bleeding and moaning she lie.
Old Mauby, Reggie and Clarkie
They hunted round the place;
The boys found poor little Hilda,
But no sign of the teacher and Grace.

Thought Mauby, the blacks might take them,
Perhaps they may spare their life;
But what sort of time would they have
At the mercy of Governor's wife.
It was true that she hated the girls,
But especially the teacher and Grace,
For they always gave her a dig
Whenever she came near the place.

Old Mauby went through the bush
Straight to the darkies' camp,
But not a soul could be seen
For the murderers had gone on the tramp.
There were two smaller boys in the house
Who hid themselves under the bed;
When Mauby came back they told him
That the teacher and Grace had fled.

Now Clarkie raced into the township,
A distance of ten miles or more,
To bring out the police and doctor.
They arrived between three and four.
The doctor looked after the wounded;
The police fossicked around,

But no sign of the girls could they see
Nor hear the slightest sound.

They took up the search again,
Just at the peep of day,
When they came on the teacher dead;
Yes, stiff and cold she lay.
This girl was fairly butchered,
She presented a terrible sight.
The position in which she was found
Proved her the victim of blackman's spite.

They all spread out in the scrub,
And there on a wallaby track
They came on the body of Grace,
Who lie stretched out on her back.
Her gown it was torn to ribbons,
She was bruised from neck to knee;
It nettled the hearts of the troopers
Such a terrible sight to see.

The ground was smeared with blood
And pieces of linen and lace,
For the hand that had handled the teacher
Had also handled Grace.
Mrs Mauby suffered much pain
And died in a day or two.
Elsie Clark recovered all right:
She was at the trial, you know.

Mrs Governor was the first they arrested,
No doubt she felt a bit wet,
Shoved all the blame on the darkies,
Turned scarey, of course, you bet.
Underwood did not reign long;
He was very soon landed in jail.
He denied Mrs Governor's yarn
And told quite a different tale.

He admitted he murdered young Mauby;

There were four of them in the swim;
There as Jimmie Governor and his wife,
Joe Governor and him.
Still Jimmie and Joe went out
And laughed at the limbs of the law—
And before they were brought to book
They murdered some four or five more.

The bloodhounds were brought from Sydney,
They started them on their tracks;
But they and the police were a failure
At catching the Breelong Blacks.
It was the civilians who brought them to justice,
And not the troopers, I vow,
For had they been left to the 'Johns'
I think they would be out now.

You pretty well know all the rest;
I haven't much more to say.
Joe Governor was shot in the bush
Just at the break of day.
But the people who live on black labour
And star at cheating the blacks
May be sure they will wipe out the debts,
If they do it with bludgeon and axe.

Jack Underwood suffered at Dubbo,
Jimmie Governor in Darlinghurst jail.
Mrs Governor got married again—
And that is the end of my tale.

J. W. KEVIN ('Arthur Ferres')

The Judge's Decision

From The Free Selector and Other Verses *(1901).*

———————

'Twas years ago on the Barcoo when flashy jockey clubs
Were few and far and far between, likewise the flashy
   pubs;
The pioneers two race-days had—the stakes were fat and
   rich,
And the meeting all a roarer was, 'twent off without a
   hitch.

The rum was strong as kerosene—'twas a hundred in the
   shade;
The dust was thick as London fog, of grass there wasn't
   a blade,
But the grimy crowd they heeded not, they came to see
   the fun,
They never brought their prads for leagues, unless to see
   them run.

They had no stand for the judge to grace, his stand was
   on the ground,
And when the handicaps were run, the crowd came
   surging round
To hear his 'verdick' straight and true, and who the
   winner was;
That crowd believed the upright judge, his word was
   Persian laws.

Their judge he was a Teuton bold, Herr Lyndorf was his
   name,
He was the local medico, a man of learned fame;

In absence of his lager dear, he drank Jamaica neat,
And never from his darkest foe would shun the welcome
treat.

'Twas now the close of the second day, the last event was
on,
The sun had set and thick the air with dust and language
strong.
It was arranged among a few Snowflake should win the
race,
But Ethiop, as black as jet, had strength and nimble pace.

Away they went, a dozen or more, 'twas flogging from
the jump,
Away they tore by mulga scrub, o'er logs and many a
stump;
The jockeys jostled, swore, and fought, 'twas each one
on his own,
And on they came 'mid prayers and dust, past rock and
tree and stone.

But now into the straight they turn, the white horse leads
them all,
The thirsty crowd begins to yell, and whoop and madly
call:
And some cry out, 'The white horse wins' and some cry
out 'The Black!'
As on they flog in straining stride adown the dusty track.

And now the black has caught the white, he creeps up
inch by inch,
But white is game and struggles on, from his place he'll
never flinch;
Again the whalebone smites the air and smites the black
horse sore,
And on they come just locked as one, amid a deafening
roar.

The judge, with duplicated sight, stood on an old
gin-case

Prepared to tell the yelling crowd the winner of the race;
He gripped the post and looked straight out where slept
   the blacks and gins,
'I swear,' said he within himself, 'I swear de first horse
   vins!'

And now again a mighty roar came wildly from the
   throng
And bets were made and threats were heard, and
   language weird and strong,
For none could tell which horse as yet should catch the
   judge's eye.
And 'White' and 'Black' and 'Black' and 'White'
   resounded through the sky.

The race is run, the stakes are won, and now the excited
   crowd
Come reeling round the upright judge and calling madly
   loud
To know which horse the winner was, for some
   'Dead-heat!' declare,
And some yell 'White', and some yell 'Black', and some
   by nothing swear.

At length the honest judge did speak, in language grim
   and cold—
'You all vos (hic) right, and you all (hic) vos wrong, you
   all vos neadly sold;
Der vinning (hic) horse he vos not (hic) vite, nor (hic)
   yet vat odders called,
Der vinner of dis (hic) handicap, he vos (hic) a tampd
   piebald!'

R. G. GLADSTONES

The Trotting Cob

Cobb and Co. coach drivers, on the route between Hay and Deniliquin in south-western New South Wales back in the nineteenth century, used to claim that a headless horseman, mounted on a trotting cob, was often to be seen at night in the vicinity of the Black Swamp. They preferred not to drive this stage of the journey alone.

R. G. Gladstones' verses are included in W. T. Pyke's The Australian Favourite Reciter *(1908).*

———————

1

Round the camp-fire we sat in the summer night,
    Watching the red embers glow;
Spinning yarns, 'talking horse', in its ruddy light;
    I remember long, long ago.

2

We had ridden all day in the burning sun
    O'er the red, scorching plain, to and fro;
For the 'super' had set us to muster the run,
    Five hundred square miles or so.

3

The supper was over, the pipes in full blast,
    When we called upon Bob for a story;
A garrulous type of the bushman was he,
    And at yarn-pitching all in his glory.

4

'Well, what shall I give you this time, boys?'
        said he,
    Turning questioning eyes round the camp.
'Oh, give us the yarn of the trotting cob,
    Who startled you at the Black Swamp.'

5

'Well, this was the way of it, boys,' said he,
    'You know that infernal old spot
Stuck right in the midst of the Old Man Plains,
    And where is the drover does not?

6

'In the winter stock route from Hay to the Murray,
    A dark and desolate camp—
I don't want to stop there again in a hurry,
    That dreary and dismal Black Swamp.

7

'We had travelled our beasts from the camp at the
        ridge,
    O'er the wide-stretching, treeless plain;
And I had the midnight watch to keep—
    And I didn't half like the game.

8

'For 'twas said that far back in the early days
    A drover camped there with his mob,
And one of his men broke his neck on the spot
    By a fall from a grey trotting cob.

9

'And every night, 'twixt twelve and one,
  His ghost returns to the swamp;
And, riding the wraith of the old grey cob,
  Rounds up all the cattle on camp.

10

'I had been on watch half an hour or so
  In the dreary and cheerless night,
When all of a sudden my horse started back,
  Snorting and quivering with fright.

11

'And well he might, for out of the gloom
  Rose the ghost of a horseman and steed,
Riding like mad, while each bullock turned
    tail,
  And scoured o'er the plain at top speed.

12

'You may bet I was scared as I rode back to camp,
  And roused the boss out of his bunk;
He wouldn't quite swallow my yarn of the ghost,
  And reckoned I'd gone and got drunk.

13

'For you know on the road not far from the place
  Was a crib where they sold fighting grog;
And he swore I had been there, and got on the
    spree;
  Bah! their liquor would stiffen a dog!

14

'As soon as the dawn broke, we got on the track
   Of the beasts—it was easy to follow,
For they had torn up the earth in their terrible rush;
   And we came on them down in the hollow.

15

'Near the bridge across the Billabong Creek
   They had stopped, and were quietly feeding;
For they had covered five miles in their headlong
      flight,
   And were heartily sick of stampeding.

16

'You would say that I lie—I'd forgive you almost,
   For it does seem a queer sort of history;
But many an old hand has seen that same ghost,
   And no one has cleared up the mystery.

17

'One thing is quite certain, old drovers maintain
   That cattle won't rest on that spot;
Whether scared by the ghost or the will-o'-the-wisp.
   Well, good-night, lads; I'm tired, if you're not.'

ARTHUR WILSON ('Dalry')

A 'Jonah' Miner

From Lays and Tales of the Mines *(1916).*

———————

One day in the early nineties, as the miners working on the afternoon shift were mustering on the surface, preparatory to going
below ground to their usual toil at one of the largest quartz mines
in the Bendigo district, Victoria, a big, raw-boned, strong-
looking man of about thirty years of age sauntered with a non-
chalant air to the open door of the changing-room, and was
immediately greeted by the shift-boss, Di Williams, with,
'Hello, Pat! Are you looking for "yacker"?'

'That I am,' replied Pat Sullivan, 'and I'll take on anything
and everything for you, Di.'

'Good! Then you can go and get candles, and I'll send down
a bit of "crib" at 8 o'clock to keep you going 'til "knock-off".
Where's Jack Thomas?' continued Di, turning to one of the tim-
bermen; 'tell him when you see him that I'm sending Pat
Sullivan with him to-night.'

'No! I'm d——d if you are! . . . Infernal Moses! Holy Peter! Do
you think I've lost my head entirely?' shouted Pat. 'I've booted
it from Wood's Point to here; I'm "hard up"—in fact "stoney"
and all but starving—but the little bit of life that's left in me I'm
sticking to. GO——MATES——WITH——JONAH——THOMAS. And
this is your friendship for me, Di Williams! Good day—and keep
your d——d job 'til I ask ye for it'; and with a look of contempt
at the bewildered shift-boss, Pat Sullivan spat disgustedly on the
ground and walked away from the mine.

. . .

Jack Thomas (better known as 'Jonah'), of Eaglehawk, Victoria,
held an unenviable record for the number of fatal accidents that
happened to miners whom he had worked mates or come into

contact with. In the long run managers experienced great difficulty in getting men to work with Thomas, and can anyone wonder at the miners' superstition in view of the following:

Jack Thomas and his three mates were engaged sinking a shaft; three of them worked below, Jack being one of the three, as he was a first-class 'driller', while the fourth man was employed in landing the stuff from the bucket.

One day one of the original party took ill and did not turn up to work, and consequently another miner was engaged, temporarily, in his place. It was considered unwise to allow the new hand to handle the stuff in the bucket above them, so it was decided that Jack Thomas should stay on top and do the 'landing'. That day, when a full bucket was nearing the top of the 150 ft. deep shaft, the winding-rope slipped through the thimble of the shackle that was attached to the bucket, and the bucket with its contents fell down the shaft and killed the three miners.

On another occasion Jack Thomas and his mate were working in a narrow drive. Jack was 'beating the drill' and putting plenty of vim into every stroke. A timberman came into the drive at that time, and seeing Jack sweating freely from his arduous work, said to him, 'Give me the hammer, Jack, and I'll tap the drill while you have a "blow",' and he thereupon took the hammer out of Thomas's hands and commenced swinging it. He had scarcely struck a dozen blows when a mass of stone fell from the roof, killing him instantly, and severely injuring the drill-holder. Jack Thomas was uninjured.

Again, the men of the early morning shift were ready and waiting to go below in their turns, and five men were huddled together in the cage that was hanging at the top of the shaft of the ――― mine, in the vicinity of Sailor's Gully, Victoria, when their descent was arrested by the manager, who had arrived on the scene, shouting, 'Don't you all know it's against the regulations for more than four men to ride in the cage! Come out of there, Thomas, – you can go down in the next cage.'

Jack Thomas got out of the cage, and immediately afterwards the cage with his mates crashed, with fatal results, downwards. The rope had broken.

HENRY E. HORNE

The Liars

At the little village of Temple Sowerby, in England's Lake District, a 'Liars' Contest' used in former times to be held on May Day each year. He who told the tallest or most absurd story was declared the winner and was given a grindstone as his prize.

The tale is told of a certain Bishop of Carlisle who, on one occasion, attended the May Day fete at Temple Sowerby. He told the villagers that it was foolish of them to hold a Liars' Contest, and concluded his solemn discourse by saying, 'For my part I have never told a lie in my life.' On hearing this, so the story goes, the judges of the competition promptly awarded first prize to the Bishop.

Henry Horne's 'The Liars' obviously owes much to that old tale. It is included in The Bulletin Book of Humorous Verses and Recitations *(1920).*

Ten boys sat in a ring and played
  At telling lies—
An Outback pastime—with a strayed
  Young dog for prize.

The Parson they informed, who strolled
  To see their fun,
'The pup was for the cove who told
  The biggest one.'

The good man looked upon that ring
  Of boys and sighed.
'I'm sorry to hear such a thing
  As this,' he cried.

'I never dared to tell a lie,
  Nor ever knew

Such sinful sport, my lads, when I
  Was young like you.'

Ten faces fell, but not from shame,
  But sheer defeat;
Ten little liars dropped the game,
  For they were beat;

Ten boys arose—a sullen band—
  Quite broken up;
And Jim, the judge, said: 'Billy, hand
  The bloke the pup.'

A. P. ROGERS

A Man From the Sea

English, American and Australian yarn-spinners have been telling the
following story for many a year.
  I have taken the Rogers version from The Bulletin Book of Humorous
Verses and Recitations *(1920).*

———————

He was a salt-encrusted man, who long had roved the
sea.
His voice was loud and raucous, his language it was
free.
He spoke of giant serpents, and of fierce, colossal
whales,
That his friend mistook for islands till they raised aloft
their tails.

At length we grew suspicious, and said we'd heard that
rum
Oft blurred the sight of sailors, whereat he shouted
'Come,
And I'll bash you into brimstone!' but we firmly
answered, 'No;
But whisper what you've seen yourself in accents soft and
low.'

'Of course,' he said, 'them mates of mine sometimes
exaggerate;
And lyin', let me tell yer, is a thing I alwus hate;
And p'raps, now that yer mention it, them blokes
imposed on me,
So I'll tell you what I've seen meself upon the blinded
sea.

'One time when we wus whalin', where the sperm an'
 humpers grow,
Right on the blazin' tropics, where the white men seldom
 go,
A native bloke informed us that no greater giants grew
Than the fish aroun' them islands—can you lend a cove
 a chew?

'So I took our longest cable, and I hooked it firm an'
 fast
To a rocky, rugged island, an' soon I made a cast,
With an anchor fer a sinker, an' I waited there an'
 smiled
A-thinkin' of me boyhood, just as happy as a child.

'But suddenly that chain went taut, an' soon a fearful
 roar
Came rumblin' through the water, rushin' towards that
 desert shore,
An' the ocean seethed an' tumbled fer quite a mile
 around.
Dog scratch me! But it puzzled me what sort uv thing
 I'd found.

'The cable jumped out tighter still, an' creaked jest like
 a winch,
But I'd hitched it to that island, an' it wouldn't budge
 an inch.
Seemed ter me I'd hooked an earthquake, an' a tidal wave
 combined,
With the heavin' sea before me, and the creakin' chain
 behind.

'Then the roarin' grew terrific, an' the groun' began ter
 heave
An' I suddenly felt giddy, an' my legs they seemed to
 leave
The shaking deck beneath me; an' the island give a
 groan,
An' jumped into the ocean, an' left me there—alone!'

A pause ensued, and moodily his beer he did assail,
And I murmured, deferentially: 'Perhaps ... it was a
    whale?'
He fixed me with his eagle eye, and scornfully did
    state,
'Great Grampus! Wot yer thinkin' of? *I used a whale for
    bait!'*

We plied him with no questions, no comments trite were
    passed.
We believe in emulation, but we saw we'd met at last
A scintillating genius in this man from out the sea,
So I rose and said politely, 'Will you have a drink with
    me?'

A. B. ('Banjo') PATERSON

The Gundaroo Bullock

From The Collected Verse of A. B. Paterson *(1921).*

Oh, there's some that breeds the Devon that's as solid as
a stone,
And there's some that breeds the brindle which they call
the 'Goulburn Roan';
But amongst the breeds of cattle there are very, very few
Like the hairy-whiskered bullock that they bred at
Gundaroo.

Far away by Grabben Gullen, where the Murrumbidgee
flows,
There's a block of broken country-side where no one ever
goes;
For the banks have gripped the squatters, and the free
selectors too,
And their stock are always stolen by the men of
Gundaroo.

There came a low informer to the Grabben Gullen side,
And he said to Smith the squatter, 'You must saddle up
and ride,
For your bullock's in the harness-cask of Morgan
Donahoo—
He's the greatest cattle-stealer in the whole of
Gundaroo.'

'Oh, ho!' said Smith, the owner of the Grabben Gullen
run,
'I'll go and get the troopers by the sinking of the sun,
And down into his homestead tonight we'll take a ride,

With warrants to identify the carcass and the hide.'

That night rode down the troopers, the squatter at their
    head,
They rode into the homestead, and pulled Morgan out
    of bed.
'Now, show to us the carcass of the bullock that you
    slew—
The hairy-whiskered bullock that you killed in
    Gundaroo.'

They peered into the harness-cask, and found it wasn't
    full,
But down among the brine they saw some flesh and bits
    of wool.
'What's this?' exclaimed the trooper; 'an infant, I
    declare';
Said Morgan, ' 'Tis the carcass of an old man native bear.
I heard that ye were coming, so an old man bear I slew,
Just to give you kindly welcome to my home in
    Gundaroo.

'The times are something awful, as you can plainly see,
The banks have broke the squatters, and they've broke
    the likes of me;
We can't afford a bullock—such expense would never
    do—
So an old man bear for breakfast is a treat in Gundaroo.'
And along by Grabben Gullen, where the rushing river
    flows,
In the block of broken country where there's no one ever
    goes,
On the Upper Murrumbidgee, they're a hospitable
    crew—
But you mustn't ask for 'bullock' when you go to
    Gundaroo.

HENRY LAWSON

Grog-an'-Grumble Steeplechase

From Poetical Works of Henry Lawson *(1925).*

'Twixt the coastline and the border lay the town of Grog-
an'-Grumble
    (Just two pubs beside a racecourse in a wilderness of
    sludge)
An' they say the local meeting was a drunken rough-and-
tumble,
    Which was ended pretty often by an inquest on the
    judge.
Yes, 'tis said the city talent very often caught a tartar
    In the Grog-an'-Grumble sportsman, 'n' retired with
    broken heads,
For the fortune, life, and safety of the Grog-an'-Grumble
starter
    Mostly hung upon the finish of the local
    thoroughbreds.

Pat M'Durmer was the owner of a horse they called The
    Screamer,
    Which he called the 'quickest shtepper 'twixt the
    Darling and the sea',
But I think it's very doubtful if a Banshee-haunted
    dreamer
    Ever saw a more outrageous piece of equine scenery;
For his points were most decided, from his end to his
    beginning;
    He had eyes of different colour, and his legs they
    wasn't mates.
Pat M'Durmer said he always came 'widin a flip av
    winnin' ',

An' his sire had come from England, 'n' his dam was
   from the States.

Friends would argue with M'Durmer, and they said he
      was in error
   To put up his horse The Screamer, for he'd lose in any
      case,
And they said a city racer by the name of Holy Terror
   Was regarded as the winner of the coming
      steeplechase;
Pat declared he had the knowledge to come in when it
      was raining,
   And irrelevantly mentioned that he knew the time of
      day,
So he rose in their opinion. It was noticed that the
      training
   Of The Screamer was conducted in a dark, mysterious
      way.

Well, the day arrived in glory, 'twas a day of jubilation
   For the careless-hearted bushmen quite a hundred
      miles around,
An' the rum 'n' beer 'n' whisky came in waggons from
      the station,
   An' the Holy Terror talent were the first upon the
      ground.
Judge M'Ard—with whose opinion it was scarcely safe
      to wrestle—
   Took his dangerous position on the bark-and-sapling
      stand:
He was what the local Stiggins used to speak of as a
      'wessel
   Of wrath', and he'd a bludgeon that he carried in his
      hand.

'Off ye go!' the starter shouted, as down fell a stupid
      jockey;
   Off they started in disorder—left the jockey where he
      lay—

And they fell and rolled and galloped down the crooked
course and rocky,
    Till the pumping of The Screamer could be heard a
    mile away.
But he kept his legs and galloped; he was used to rugged
courses,
    And he lumbered down the gully till the ridge began
    to quake:
And he ploughed along the sidling, raising earth till other
horses
    An' their riders, too, were blinded by the dust-cloud
    in his wake.

From the ruck he'd struggle slowly—they were much
    surprised to find him
    Close abeam of Holy Terror as along the flat they
    tore—
Even higher still and denser rose the cloud of dust behind
    him,
    While in more divided splinters flew the shattered
    rails before.
'Terror!' 'Dead heat!' they were shouting—'Terror!' but
    the Screamer hung out
    Nose to nose with Holy Terror as across the creek they
    swung,
An' M'Durmer shouted loudly, 'Put yer tongue out, put
    yer tongue out!'
    An' The Screamer put his tongue out, and he won by
    half-a-tongue.

EDWARD HARRINGTON

'There's Only Two of Us Here'

From The Kerrigan Boys and Other Australian Verses *(1944)*.

I camped one night in an empty hut on the side of
    a lonely hill;
I didn't go much on empty huts, but the night was
    awful chill.
So I boiled me billy and had me tea, and seen that
    the door was shut,
Then I went to bed in an empty bunk by the side of
    the old slab hut.

It must have been about twelve o'clock—I was feeling
    cosy and warm—
When at the foot of me bunk I see a horrible ghostly
    form.
It seemed in shape to be half an ape with a head like
    a chimpanzee,
But wot the 'ell was it doin' there, and wot did it
    want with me?

You may say if you please that I had d.ts. or call me
    a crimson liar,
But I wish you had seen it as plain as me with its eyes
    like coals of fire!
Then it gave a moan and a horrible groan that curdled
    me blood with fear,
And, 'There's only two of us here,' it ses; 'there's only
    two of us here!'

I kept one eye on the old hut door and one on the
    awful brute;

I only wanted to dress meself and get to the door
    and scoot.
But I couldn't find where I'd left me boots so I hadn't
    a chance to clear;
And, 'There's only two of us here,' it moans, 'there's
    only two of us here!'

I hadn't a thing to defend meself, not even a stick
    or stone;
And, 'There's only two of us here!' it ses again with
    a horrible groan.
I thought I'd better make some reply, though I
    reckoned me end was near:
'By the holy smoke, when I finds me boots there'll be
    only one of us here!'

I gets me hands on me number tens and out through
    the door I scoots,
And I lit the whole of the hillside up with the sparks
    from me blucher boots.
So I've never slept in a hut since then, and I tremble
    and shake with fear
When I think of that horrible form wot moaned,
    'There's only two of us here!'

ANONYMOUS

The Phantom Bullocky

From Smith's Weekly *(16 April, 1949).*

It will be obvious to many Australian readers that the story which follows is a variant of Lance Skuthorpe's 'The Champion Bullock-Driver'.

Suggested further reading: Bill Wannan, A Treasury of Australian Humour *(1960).*

I was boss on Thurloona at the time.

The chap who wanted a job was of the all-round run of bush-men, and as I needed a bullock-driver I gave him a try-out. I told him that the team he would have to handle was one of eight-yoke, with the wildest cattle in Australia in it, and showed him the graves of fourteen men killed at one time and another by the oxen.

'I'll try 'em,' he said.

I asked him if he had the language. He said that often when he had been bogged in the timber his conversation had set the stringy bark trees on fire—not the big ones, but the saplings.

I told him he might suit, and asked him to give me an example of himself starting a team.

'You take eight panels of the fence of the yard,' I said. 'Imagine that's your team, and get 'em going.' The eight panels of the yard were new timber, big posts, each with four strands of galvanized wire run through and tied to a four-foot stringy bark. He said it would do him.

I handed him a whip—the same the fourteen dead bullockies had used in turn. The handle was 6 foot, the lash 18 foot of plaited greenhide; and there was 2 foot of silk cracker. He bent the handle over his knee in two or three places, to test it for flaws, then ran the lash slowly through his hand as if feeling it for a loose strand.

Then he started the team. He walked along and tapped each post with the butt of the handle, as a hint to the bullocks to tighten the chains. Then he gave a cheer, the whip kept cracking, and presently a little blue flame ran along the top wire of the fence. He kept on exhorting the bullocks and cheering loudly. The flame danced along the wire, and the whip cracking sounded like the Day of Judgement.

When the outfit fairly started, he cheered like ten thousand, and, to my amazement, the fourteen graves opened, and the fourteen killed bullockies jumped out, each carrying a whip. They walked right up to the new man. When he saw them he gave another and louder cheer, and the fourteen phantoms hailed him as the King of the Bullockies. All together the fifteen whips fell on the top wire, and the flame ran up and down as if it were alive.

Then the posts began to walk forward step by step, straining on the wires. Then the drivers gave a louder cheer than ever, talked faster and louder, and the team strained in the yokes until the four-foot stringy bark tree came out of the ground and fell in behind. The driver that I had hired cheered wildly, and kept on going up the hill with the tree. The others gave him a cheer as he disappeared, and all rushed back and jumped into their graves.

He went round the foot of the hill and came back. 'I think I could drive your team,' he said to me.

I said, 'You can have the job. You're the best man with a fence that I ever saw.'

Then he laughed, gave another cheer, and jumped up in the air. He never came down again.

GORDON WILLIAMS

Haunted Hills

*Gordon Williams, a distinguished Melbourne journalist, retold a number
of old Australian ghost stories for readers of the* Argus Magazine *during
the year 1951. Included in the series were the two tales which follow. The
Haunted Hills are in the Gippsland region of eastern Victoria.*

———————

Moe slumbered beneath a benevolent end-of-winter sun. The atmosphere was drowsy, and the barman and the storekeeper, who
leaned idly against the jamb of the hotel door, spoke only fit-
fully.

'Sometimes,' said Phil the storekeeper, 'I think I'll get out of
this place. Too quiet.'

'Yeh. What'd you do? Go lookin' for gold with the rest of the
bunch 'round Clunes?'

'Maybe. Might even go down to Melbourne. Might even go
to sea. Some nice full-riggers in there now. Always wanted to
go to sea.'

'Why didn't you?'

'I get seasick.'

'Oh.'

Talk fell away.

'Maybe I'd better get back to the bar,' said Ben.

'What for?'

'Dunno really. No quieter in there than it is out here... Got
an idea you'd better stay in these parts, though. Lot o' money
to be made here, y'know. Bloke down at Cassidy's the other night
was saying there's coal round about.'

'Yeh? A coal man?'

'No. He's one of those whatty'-callems. A divine, or something.'

'A diviner. Lot o' nonsense. Gets a bit o' stick and the stick
jumps up and down, and he says it's diamonds, or coal, or gold.

As if a stick would know. Full of spooks and goblins like those Fox Sisters. No truck with such things myself. . . Ah, well. . .'

'Better be goin',' said Ben.

'Me, too. Damn town's so quiet you could—'

Phil broke off suddenly.

'Cloud o' dust making up pretty big over there, Ben.'

'Yeh. . . Lot o' noise, too.'

'Cattle.'

'Must be comin' quick if it is. Never saw cattle comin' that fast.'

The two men turned toward the east. A dustcloud bellied up, took grotesque form.

A low rumbling crescendoed into a roar.

Then it was upon the town . . . a herd of wild, red-eyed cattle.

Phil and Ben gaped.

'Look at 'em goin'!' breathed Phil. 'Whoever's drivin' them cattle is doin' a job, orright. Whose herd is it?'

'How'd I know? Let's wait and see who's proddin' 'em.'

The herd raced past. The street was filled with dust, and dirt, and the acrid smell of sweat-soaked hides bit into the consciousness of those who had crowded out to watch the pageantry of racing beasts.

'Stampede,' said Phil, laconically.

'Wi' the devil behind 'em,' said Ben.

They waited till the last beast had vanished into the west. . . waited for the stockman who was pressing them on.

But there was no stockman.

And there never was a stockman. . .

'Listen,' said Phil to the half packed bar. 'Those cattle came through a week ago. Stands to reason there must ha' been a drover somewhere. Where'd he go? Where'd the cattle come from? Where. . .'

'Came down from the hills,' said Cassidy. 'Anyway, maybe we should go up there and see if some bloke's hurt or somethin'. Musta been a drover there in the first place.'

The talk grew.

A party set off to the hills, searched around. . .

They found a blackened campfire. There were signs that

men—perhaps three—had camped there. Around the fire were dead beasts, stiffened into ugliness. There was broken bush, churned earth. . .

But neither then nor since was there ever a sign of the drover, nor ever a sign to tell what made the maddened beasts come driving down out of the rises.

So began the legend of Gippsland's Haunted Hills. . .

It was a few years later when a white-faced man told his story.

'I was camped up there for the night,' he said. 'I'd got a good sort of fire goin', and it was as cosy as all get-out. I was just goin' to caulk off when I heard whips crackin' the other side of the hill.

' "Drovers," I said, "and a funny time to be drovin'. Should ha' had those cattle bedded down long ago." So I go over the rise to see what's up. And I hear the voices and the whips and the hooves. . . But there's no one there. No one, I tell y'. I can see the whole place clear as noonday, the moon bein' big an' all, but there's no one.'

'What did you do?' asked the tall man from Geelong, who was out on company business.

'What w'd you ha' done? I got movin' fast as I could . . . but there was lead in me shoes . . . I came out of that place fast as I could, lemme tell you . . . I've got to go back for me swag—but I'll go back in daylight.'

'Nonsense', said the man from Geelong. 'You were dozing in front of your fire, and the rest was all in your mind.'

'I never 'ad a mind like that before,' said the tale-teller. 'I bin in funny places, too. Once I camped in a cemetery, and another time I brought in two corpses out o' the Murray, but I didn't get any mind trouble then. . . Maybe you'd like to go up there?'

'Pleasure,' said the man from Geelong.

And he went.

But he came back before the night of his vigil was four hours old.

He said very little. But to Phil the barman he confided that he didn't want to go into the hills again.

'There are too many blackfellows there,' he said.

And Phil scratched his head wonderingly.

He hadn't heard of blackfellows up there. . .

By this time, the legend of the Haunted Hills was big with suggestion, menace, and, of course, variety. . .

There were travellers who had seen a ghostly stockman driving a phantom herd; there were others who had seen blackfellows in corroboree—but silently, eerily.

It became difficult to sift fact from imagination.

There were many theories . . . innumerable theories.

But, in the popular mind, the Haunted Hills remained a haunted place.

I heard the story long ago, in all its variations, and paid little attention to it.

Then, one day, newspaper business took me down to the Moe-Traralgon area.

I had driven through the hills one night, without realizing that I was near 'haunted' ground. On the way I had given a lift to a wayfarer. It was when we were coming down the farthest slope of the hills that he turned to me and said:

'That bloke couldn't have seen us coming.'

'What bloke?' I asked.

'The fellow on the horse, of course,' he said. 'I thought you were going to go right through him.'

'I didn't see a bloke on a horse,' I said, a little bewildered.

'You didn't?' His voice held a little scorn. 'You must ha' been asleep.'

'What did he look like, then?'

'Bloke with a stockwhip. Big felt hat. Turn round and you'll see him plain enough.'

I had as many doubts about my companion's eyesight as he obviously had about mine.

That night I mentioned the affair to a friend of mine—a business man—in Traralgon.

'That's funny,' he said, 'but not particularly unusual. Lot of people round here talk of the Stockman, or the Drover. Probably it's something developed out of their subconscious. They've heard so many stories about the Haunted Hills that when they pass through them they expect to see the Unseeable . . . and, with the inner eye of their minds, they see it.

'A sort of moonshine madness, I suppose.'

. . .

I thought so, too.

But an old, old woman near Koo-wee-rup remembered the drover who disappeared.

She told me that the hills held a blackfellows' burial ground . . . an interdicted burial ground . . . a place of tabu.

I remembered her age, respected her sincerity, but felt the story was still just a piece of folklore.

I was told, by a very matter-of-fact professional man in the agricultural service, that animals would not stay on the 'haunted hills' at night.

I checked on this; many people supported it. Others denied it.

But—

'I think it is true,' the professional man told me. 'I was riding through there once in the daytime, and my horse became rigid with fright. . . Don't ask me why. I got him moving and out of there as fast as I could. And I'm not imaginative.'

Further investigation (by this time I was interested more than, as Runyon would say, somewhat) revealed what might have been a theory.

'These hills were underlaid by brown coal. It was burnt out in some subterranean fire. Since then the hills have been hollow, and give off strange sounds to the acute animal ear.'

. . .

There you have it.

In the first place, there are many reliable witnesses to testify to the appearance of a 'drover'.

There are many others who have seen herds of cattle where no cattle were known to be.

There are others who speak of 'crowds of blackfellows'.

Are they all wrong?

Are we up against another instance of mass imagination, mass hypnotism?

The ribbon road of bitumen cutting through the hills now, and the prosaic pattern of motor traffic have broken down the legend of the place.

But—and I am assured of this by those who should know—no beast roams those hills now, nor will.

Well, there's the story.

Right or wrong, normal or supernormal, I hope it has been worth the telling.

GORDON WILLIAMS

A White Bull Came Mourning

The first authentic account of the sighting of the while bull by four police officers of the Queanbeyan and Yass districts of New South Wales, on a day in 1876, was given by Martin Brennan, ex-Senior Superintendent, in Reminiscences of the Gold Fields *(1907). Brennan was an eye-witness to the events he described. The strange tale has been retold many times. I gave it an airing in my book,* Legendary Australians *(1974).*

'Well, that's that,' sighed Police Superintendent Martin Brennan, of Yass and Queanbeyan. The last spadeful of drought-dry earth had fallen upon the mound that rose above poor, murdered McCarthy, the humble, religious, slightly pathetic shepherd who had for so long tended Davis's sheep along the Murrumbidgee.

'McCarthy never injured man or beast, and there's going to be no rest for any policeman in this district until the man that finished him off is picked up.'

'A terrible business, indeed,' Trooper McIntosh murmured, 'and never a sign who 'twas that blew off the gun into the poor mannie's head and then carved half of his skull with a sheath or some other knife and———.'

'All right, Mac.' Brennan was terse. 'We heard enough of the gory details at the inquest. And though it's a case of murder by some person or persons unknown, it's not going to stop that way.'

'The coroner wouldn't let me say it in court, but I can tell you who to look for.'

Brennan turned to the quiet man beside him who stood almost in the shade of the murdered man's crude log cabin.

'Yes, Mr Davis? Well, speak up, then. Remember, suspicions never hanged anybody, though.'

'I think you should start looking for Tom Robinson.'

'That hell-hound? We've been trying to get the drop on that fellow for a dozen things . . . Tom the Soldier, they call him; Waterloo Tom . . . but tell me now. Has he been around the Washpen here at all?'

'He has been, as I could have told you before, had I been let. The night before poor McCarthy was murdered I found the ruffian in my kitchen. I gave him a shakedown. I noticed he had a gun with a barrel six feet long if it was an inch. "Long Tom", he called it.'

'Did he know McCarthy?'

'He asked me where Mac was . . . if he was still at the Washpen. I told him he was, and next morning when I came out I could see no sign of Robinson. He must ha' cleared out early . . . and funnily enough I missed a can of strychnine, and one of my left-foot boots.'

'Any bad blood between him and McCarthy?'

'Not that I know of. But Robinson wouldn't have to be in bad blood to kill a man. He's just a low fiend. Crazy. A born ———.'

'I know his record.' Superintendent Brennan thought a while. 'Lagged out from England to Van Diemen's Land . . . lived with the Aborigines . . . kidnapped young lubras. He migrated to New South Wales when his time was up . . . tramped about the country, boasting of his prowess as a soldier and a marksman, always talking about the thousands he'd killed in battle. Lived on birds, possums, kangaroos; prowled at night, robbed, purloined, terrorized . . . Maybe he's behind the story of a few missing men on our files. I wouldn't be surprised. A maniac, I'd say.'

'There's your man, then. Oughtn't to be hard to catch up with him. He's six foot four, gangling, his ears flap, and that beard of his makes his face as murderous as Bloody Morgan's. You should ———.'

'We know him, all right. And we'll get him. But will we get the evidence? That's the point.'

'I think you will,' said Mr Davis quietly.

The hunt began. Through the drought-stricken Yass-Queanbeyan area the police moved up and down in a gauntly brown country. Everything seemed to be burnt out . . . the grass, the creeks, and even the cattle that once roamed the bush . . .

'Not even a beastie about to break the monotony,' complained Trooper McIntosh, on patrol.

'Seems unreal. Always find a few cows about to make things more friendly like on a ride like this. Poor McCarthy was very fond of 'em. Almost as fond of 'em as he was of his sheep. Always had one hanging around his hut, poor bloke.'

It was then that the police found the missing piece of McCarthy's skull.

New search of his cabin unearthed a can of strychnine—the one supposedly taken from Davis's by Robinson; then a left-foot boot . . .

Robinson's lair in a hollow log near Duntroon was discovered. . . Robinson was nearby. Robinson and Long Tom. . . He fired. . . and fired again. This time his aim was bad. Tom was taken after a sharp struggle.

'Why,' asked Brennan, 'did you want to shoot us? You know the others would have got you. . .'

'I've shot thousands in battle,' boasted Tom the Soldier. 'It's got that way now that I can't see a man passing without wanting to make a target of him. . .'

Tom was wearing left-foot boots. And his blankets were those once used by McCarthy.

So far, it was a plain, if horrible, story of cold-blooded, maniacal murder.

But then it became necessary to open McCarthy's grave to recover blankets placed there with the body: one was the blanket Tom Robinson had stolen from Davis.

Superintendent Brennan, Inspector Brennan, a trooper from Yass, and Trooper McIntosh went to the Washpen on a 'beautiful clear day', when 'everything seemed still in the locality save the sheoaks, which gave out doleful murmurs in the zephyr. The sun's rays shone upon the serpentine windings of the river. . .'

But suddenly, dramatically all this was changed:

'Scarcely,' wrote Superintendent Brennan, 'had we stood beside the grave when an extraordinary cumulo-stratus cloud, or woolpack, descended and enveloped the Washpen in comparative darkness. . .'

The party was a little shaken, but the work of exhumation went on.

Then, just as the digging trooper's spade touched the slab that covered McCarthy's body the ground rocked to the force of a terrific explosion . . . the earth seemed to ripple, sink, then heave.

'My God!' shouted McIntosh. 'It's a thunderbolt, or an earthquake!'

There came an awesome, rumbling roar that filled the entire valley with an eerie sound.

The police party were shattered. . . In the midday darkness, they knew, they felt, that here was no natural phenomenon. They crowded together waiting . . . waiting . . . but for what?

None knew afterward.

Then from the mountain top that reared above them there came one long, thunderous roar. It echoed and fell and rose along the walls of the valley until it seemed that the ears could no longer receive its volume, or sense resist its impact.

Then, just as suddenly, came quiet . . . a quiet that was more terrifying than the hell-roars of a moment ago.

Silence that could be felt, that wrapped itself around a man's limbs, holding him motionless in the middle of a nightmare.

'Look there!' whispered McIntosh. 'Look there. . . My God, see how it comes!'

And through the gloom—gloom in midday—a huge bull, immaculately white, its eyes blazing and its feet throwing aside earth and pebble, came charging. . . Came charging . . . but no hoofbeat sounded.

For a while the police party stood paralysed. Then fear finally set them running to the shelter of trees, revolvers drawn.

But the great white bull passed them by. . . It raced to the grave, silently, intently. There it stopped motionless.

With head erect it surveyed the country around, pawed the earth furiously, but all in deadly silence, moaned piteously, fell. . .

And there, by the open grave of McCarthy the Shepherd, McCarthy the animal lover, it died.

After a while the police party came out. They glanced at the great carcase without approaching it. The fear of the supernatural held them all; but there was no life in the great white body. The great red eyes were open and dead. There was no breath.

'Come,' whispered Inspector Brennan. 'Let's finish this

ghoul's job and get out of this.'

Two days later Trooper McIntosh, under orders, was sent again
to the Washpen grave. Trooper McIntosh was almost insubordi-
nate about his errand. But as he was on his way he was joined
by Mr Davis, who was eager to see the extraordinary white bull.
He was frankly sceptical. He even joked a little about police
credulity. . .

And when McIntosh and Davis reached the grave there was
no sign of the bull, no hoof marks in the dry soil, no indication
that any save booted men had set foot there.

McIntosh was amazed.

'Nobody could have made off with that great carcase without
carving it up,' he said. 'And if it had been carved there would
have been signs of it. . . That bull came at us all right, Mr Davis.
And it came without making any sound. And the darkness of that
cloud—that awful roaring and rocking and blasting—I'll remember it to my dying day.'

But Davis only smiled.

Now let Superintendent Brennan take up the tale:

'I am well aware that assertions regarding ghosts, apparitions,
and mysterious manifestations create a smile. The parties who
allege they have seen or experienced them are looked upon by
self-constituted wiseacres as weak minded, silly, and superstitious ignoramuses, whose movements require strict surveil-
lance.

'In the present case I merely describe what four police officers, in perfect health, and with all their faculties unimpaired,
saw and carefully observed in the day-time, and what, after
many years' service in the police force, they were unable to
account for. Hence they regard the occurrence as a psychological
phenomenon.'

Partly because of counsel's plea that Robinson was insane, Tom
the Soldier was sentenced to life imprisonment. He did not ap-
preciate having been saved from the gallows, but raved continu-
ously. Every day he claimed that he was being tortured by fiends,
that women, each of whom claimed to be his wife, inflicted terrible punishment upon him.

And then . . . he began to shout that he was being trampled to death by a great, white bull.

There was no escape from the bull, he said.

He tried to commit suicide.

But he could not escape the bull that way, either.

He died after suffering as few men have suffered . . . died, as he fancied, beneath the trampling hooves of a great white bull that only he could see.

. . .

That is the story of the strange events that attended the Washpen Murder of 1876.

Every fact is recorded without drama or conscious effect-seeking by Senior-Superintendent Martin Brennan, for forty-eight years an officer of police; Inspector Brennan, Trooper McIntosh, and other police officers confirmed the superintendent's account.

No one could explain the great white bull.

There was not, there never had been, any such animal in the district.

Why did it come to McCarthy's grave? Why did it come in the terror of earthquake and ghastly, inexplicable roaring—a roaring that was not heard outside the valley?

Why? And how?

And why did it come to Robinson's delirium?

I have told the tale truly—but the answer does not rest in it.

GREG RUSSELL

The Man They Couldn't Sack

The late Greg Russell, rodeo showman extraordinary, often sent me stories he'd collected from bush workers on his journeys across Australia. 'The Man They Couldn't Sack' was one of them; and I printed it in my 'Come in Spinner' column in Australasian Post *(16 October 1958). It is, of course, reminiscent of Henry Lawson's sketch, 'Mitchell Doesn't Believe in the Sack'; but I have no doubt that Greg Russell picked it up while yarning with shearers at one of the outback sheds. It's the kind of tale that will continue to have relevance as long as mankind is divided up into bosses and workers.*

The changeover from blade to machine shearing, at the beginning of the present century, brought with it many problems of human adjustment to the new method.

This is the story of a shearer with such a problem.

In the early days of the century there lived in western New South Wales a station owner who was known far and wide as 'Hungry Smith'. So mean was this man that it was his habit to give his children threepence each in the evening if they'd go to bed without their tea. Then, in the morning, he'd demand the money back or they'd get no breakfast. At any rate, that is what his neighbours said about Hungry Smith.

Shearing was in full swing at Smith's station one season; and as he'd recently installed machine shears it was his rule to keep a close check on each shearer to ensure that he was getting the hang of the new implements. Should his eagle eye note any sheep that was improperly shorn, he'd place a raddle mark on the animal's back and the shearer wouldn't be paid for that one.

Now old Bill the shearer had learned his craft on the blades; and that he was having a hard time with the machine shears was to say the least. Bill had just finished a wether when Smith step-ped up, placed a raddle mark on the animal's back, and said bluntly, 'Now, Bill, if you don't make a better job of that next one you'd better roll your swag.'

Bill belonged to the old school of shearers who believed that if you weren't chipped by the boss at least once a day you were falling down on the job. So he smiled and said amiably, 'Right-o, Mr Smith'.

The next sheep was worse shorn than the previous one. On went the raddle mark, and Smith said, 'All right, Bill, you're sacked. Come to the house after dinner and draw your time.' Smith turned on his heel and went out to the yards to help with the drafting.

Old Bill wasn't the sort to give up easily, so he just continued to shear. After dinner Smith came into the shed to see where Bill was. He almost threw a blue fit when he saw the old-timer serenely shearing a wether.

'Hey!' Smith bellowed, 'I thought I sacked you this morn-ing.'

Bill gave him a silly grin and said, 'Yes, boss.'

'Well, pack your gear and come down to the house and take your cheque—and *get going!*'

Smith made off for the house. When Bill hadn't arrived within half an hour he hurried back to the shed. He turned up just in time to see old Bill shove a shorn wether down the chute. Smith almost foamed at the mouth as he screamed, 'You're *sacked*, I tell you! Now get off the board and don't come back!'

Smith wasn't going to be fooled again, so he removed the hand-piece that Bill had been using. He got some wire and put a bullocky twitch around the gate of Bill's catching pen so that it couldn't be opened. Then he took a hammer, some nails and a couple of bits of timber and boarded in the old-timer's chute.

To make doubly sure that Bill was finished, Smith spoke to each shearer in turn, warning that if he helped Bill in any way he'd be sacked as well.

Hungry Smith turned to the forlorn-looking old Bill and said, 'It's a bit late in the day for you to leave now. You can stay the night. *But you must be gone by the morning.*' Old Bill managed a grin and said, 'Yes, boss.'

Next morning Smith was up early; and before work had begun in the shearing shed he had gone to muster one of the back paddocks, accompanied by two stockmen.

Meanwhile, old Bill walked to the shearing shed. He looked at his wired-up pen, inspected the boarded chute, and decided he was beaten on the board. He picked up his tool bag and slowly walked outside.

Bill stood by the sheep yards and took one last look. He turned to leave. Then he saw three sheets of corrugated iron leaning against the shearing shed wall. He smiled. Hurriedly gathering up the iron he carried it into one of the yards where the sheep were. Soon he had a makeshift shelter propped up beside the rails. Then from out of his tool bag he took a pair of shears and a sharpening stone. He applied the stone to the blades and when he was satisfied with the edges he put them carefully down and caught a sheep.

All morning old Bill toiled beneath his shelter and by dinner-time he had a considerable number shorn. When the other shearers came out for their midday meal they saw what old Bill was doing and smiled, but said nothing.

After dinner, Bill was back at it again, taking the wool off with his shears. Around three o'clock Hungry Smith and the two stockmen returned to the yards with the fresh mob. They'd yarded these sheep before Smith at last saw Bill working with the blades.

Smith let out a bellow of rage, jumped two fences, and fairly flew to where the old-timer was toiling. He stood speechless, shaking with anger.

Then a change came over the station owner as he began to see the humour of the situation. First he smiled. Then came chortles, followed by bursts of uncontrollable laughter. Tears ran down his face. He sank down on his knees, then lay in the dust of the yard, helpless in his mirth.

Hungry Smith gained control of himself. Getting to his feet he put a hand on Bill's shoulder. 'You can have your stand back,' he said.

Bill wasted no time getting on with his job; and Hungry Smith left him, a cheerful smile on his usually grim face.

From that day on, Hungry Smith was a changed man; and a lot of his meanness left him. True, if the neighbours are to be believed, he'd still give his kids threepence apiece if they'd go to bed without their tea. But in the morning, instead of demanding the money back, he'd allow them to keep it—and still eat their breakfast.

BILL WANNAN

Crooked Mick and the Man From Big Burrawong

*Crooked Mick of the Speewah was the Paul Bunyan of the old-time Queensland shearers and shed hands*мthat is, he was a larger-than-life work hero who could shear faster, shoot straighter, fight more scientifically, even cook a better damper, than anyone else within cooee.

I have discussed the origins of Crooked Mick in a book which has long been out of print, and from which the following extract has been taken: Crooked Mick of the Speewah and Other Tall Tales *(1965)*.

Crooked Mick only once met a man who could match him in skill and endurance, and even outsmart him at times. Here's the story of their encounter.

At high noon one day, Mick rode up to the Speewah Arms Hotel, tied his horse, and strolled into the bar.

'Give me a dozen pots!' he said to the barman, Honest Joe.

Mick was then in his prime, without an ounce of fat. Knocking off the dozen pots, he said 'Fill 'em up again!'

After downing these he leaned back on the bar counter and filled his pipe. Honest Joe looked worried. 'They tell be Big Barnett of the Burrawong is headin' this way, lookin' for a fight,' he muttered.

'I've heard a lot about this Big Barnett,' said Crooked Mick cheerfully. 'I'd like to meet him. I'm as fit as a Mallee bull. He can try his fists on me any time he likes.'

With that, a little weed of a fellow walked up and intervened. 'I wouldn't say that if I was you, mate. You'd better keep out of Big Barnett's way if you value your skin. He's a helluva lot bigger than you. They say he's the biggest bloke on Big Burrawong—and that's sayin' somethin'!'

Big Burrawong, which adjoins the eastern boundary of the Speewah, is said by those who ought to know, to be the largest station property in the world. One of my informants tells me that as recently as last year the Boss of Big Burrawong had to hire two extra rouseabouts and a speedboat to skim the fat off the soup for the shearers' mess. It is also common knowledge that the Boss of Big Burrawong wanted to hire the Sydney Harbour for last year's shearing, but the authorities wouldn't have it. They knew that he was stuck for water, but they reckoned he'd get the Harbour mixed up with his dams and send the wrong one back. Then they wouldn't know if they were living in Sydney or Melbourne or not.

Anyway, when Crooked Mick heard what the little weed of a fellow had to say he threw back his head and laughed. 'Let him come!' he roared. 'He don't scare me.'

Next thing, they looked out and saw a cloud of dust approaching the pub. It turned out to be a mighty man, twice the size of Crooked Mick. He sat astride a crocodile and whipped it along with a seven-foot taipan.

On reaching the pub the huge bloke tied the crocodile to a verandah post with the taipan, hurried in, and ordered a bucket of scotch. His muscles rippled like bladders of lard in a high wind as he knocked the scotch off and then said to the barman, 'Fill her up again—and hurry!'

Crooked Mick realized that he was done. He was no opponent for this giant. So he reached up and tapped the whisky drinker on the chest.

'I've got an apology to make to you, mate,' he said.

But the big bloke cut him short. 'Sorry I can't wait to hear it,' he said nervously. 'I'm orf. I hear Big Barnett of the Burrawong is headin' in this direction lookin' for a fight—and he hates my flamin' insides. See you some other time.'

The mighty stranger rushed out, mounted the crocodile, and whipped it into a gallop with the taipan. They had soon disappeared over the horizon in a cloud of dust.

Well, Crooked Mick began to feel a bit worried. And presently a dust storm blew up from the east; and out of the gloom raced a twelve-ton territory buffalo with a gigantic man astride it, whipping it along with a seven-foot crocodile. He rode straight up to the Speewah Arms and jumped to the ground, causing the pub to tilt over at an angle of fifteen degrees. He was three times the size of Crooked Mick; and he had to crawl on hands and knees to get through the doorway into the bar-room.

'Bring me a forty-four gallon drum of wood alcohol!' he roared to Honest Joe. Then he looked around. 'I hear,' he said, 'that some over-grown peewit around these parts wants to fight me?'

'Well,' admitted Crooked Mick uneasily, 'I did—but I don't now.'

Big Barnett (for that's who the stranger was) looked down at Mick and laughed, shattering a couple of window panes. 'I don't fight boys!' he rumbled. 'Why, I could pick you up and throw you that far that when you came down it'd be Christmas time next year.'

Crooked Mick didn't dispute this information.

'But I'll tell you what I'll do,' continued Big Barnett a little more amiably, as the wood alcohol began to warm his veins. 'I'll try you out in a shearing contest.'

'Right-o,' said Mick. 'That's more in my line.'

Referees were appointed and a thousand hoggets were yarded and penned. Machine shearing was just coming into vogue at the time, so each contestant was supplied with a handpiece, and a large barrel of water to cool it in.

By evening, both men had run out of hoggets; and a thousand more were yarded and penned. All through the night they shore—and by morning there was so much wool about that prices crashed in London.

At last the referees declared in favour of Big Barnett. He was moving so fast, as it happened, that when the verdict was announced he shore an extra five hoggets before he could pull up.

Crooked Mick was dissatisfied with the outcome of this shearing duel. He proposed to Big Barnett that they should engage in a tale-telling contest.

'Right,' said the man from Big Burrawong, 'you can lead off.'

'Well,' began Crooked Mick, 'I had a sheep dog once—Lassie was her name—and she was the cleverest dog you ever saw. She used to train her pups herself. I sneaked down one time and watched how she did it. She had a row of bottles, and five of the pups were working blowflies and rounding them into the bottles.

'The sixth pup had five corks; and as each of the others yarded its blowie, the little fellow would pop a cork in the bottle. Yes, Lassie was certainly clever, the way she taught them pups!'

'That story's as stale as yesterday's beer,' growled Big Barnett. 'Now *I* had a dog once and he was outstanding. He could do everything except talk. Terry was his name . . . little fox terrier he was.

'Terry had a bad habit of sleeping on my bunk while I was away, and I didn't like it because he always left some of his dog-fleas there. Well, I tried all kinds of ways of punishing him, but it didn't make any difference. He got real cunning; and whenever he heard me coming he'd jump off the bed.

'I caught up on that trick, of course, because I could feel the warm place on my bunk where Terry'd been lying. And then I'd punish him some more.

'But one day I came in unexpectedly—and d'ya know what that clever little bastard was doing? He was on his hind legs beside the bunk, *blowing on the warm spot to cool it down!*'

There was silence for a few minutes while the referees allotted their points. Then they signalled Crooked Mick to begin the second round.

Mick said: 'I've been in some pretty thick dust storms in me time, but nothing like the one I struck between here and the Paroo a couple of years back. I had a mob of sheep that had to be brought over to the Speewah in a terrible hurry; and I knew that if I waited for the dust storm to settle I'd lose a few days. So there was only one thing to do—I jest drove the mob right over it. That'll give you some idea how thick it was.'

'I don't know about thick dust,' said Big Barnett, 'but I *have* had experience of thick fog. I was out rabbiting with a mate on the Whopperloo Creek one time. Just after we made camp, about three o'clock in the afternoon, a heavy fog came down, Well, that same night I left me mate in the tent while I went off to set the traps. The fog was that thick I couldn't see me own hand, even with a hurricane lamp. I put down an open set of traps every twenty yards or so; and then I had to find me way back to camp by coo-eeing to me mate.

'That night, I remember, me and me mate talked of nothing but that fog—and of the feed of rabbit we'd have next morning.

'When daylight came the fog lifted. We set out to see what

the luck of the night had brought us. We came to the first trap. It was set all right, but not under the ground, nor was its peg driven inter the earth.

'Mystified, we moved on to the next trap. It was lying on top of the ground, just like the first. We continued on and not one trap had a peg in the ground or under the dirt.

'Suddenly, the solution to this mystery dawned on me. The fog had been so thick during the night that in planting the traps I'd scratched holes in the fog, driven pegs into them—*and covered each set over with fog!*'

In the third round, Mick began: 'When I was tree-fellin', about thirty years ago, I used to use a 52-pound double-headed axe so that I could cut down two trees at the same time. One big tree I felled was so tall we got seven hundred posts out of it. And you mightn't believe this, but when I went back to that spot twenty years later, people were still picking up the chips.'

'If you're talking of axemen,' said Big Barnett, 'I reckon I know the greatest man of all time. Young Wompah Wallace of Nar Nar Goon. He's real good—would've been a champeen if he hadn't gone an' tangled with a circular saw and lost both arms . . . about three or four years ago, it was.

'Anyway, I was at the Burramugga Show last year and I seen them all line up for the horizontal log chop. And who should be in that line-up but young Wompah! He was sort of sitting on his axe-handle, waiting for the word Go.

'At the pistol shot he sprang inter the air and started turning somersaults and his axe was flashing in the sun like a windmill. Lovely to watch, it was. Every time it came round it bit a piece out of that log as big as a cabbagetree hat. It was really pretty to see young Wompah turn in the air to tackle the opposite side of the log. He run out winner by ten seconds. . .'

'Wait a minute,' Crooked Mick interrupted, 'that's a lousy lie if ever there was one! How could he hold his axe with no arms?'

Big Barnett looked thoughtfully at Mick for a few moments, then said, 'Look, young Wompah will be chopping again at the next Burramugga Show. Why don't you go down and see for yerself?'

The judges of the contest decided that they'd heard enough. They totted up their tallies and announced that Big Barnett was the winner by 2,974 points.

The two contestants adjourned to the pub for refreshment; and before long Big Barnett was reminiscing about his hunting days.

'I was out after buffalo one time,' he recalled, 'and I had the most incredible bad luck that can be imagined. Every time I had a shot something went wrong and I missed. By the afternoon I was clean out of ammo. And still empty-handed.

'I decided to give the game away; but as I was walking home along the track a big red 'roo hopped out of the scrub and sat up—a perfect target—about two miles in front of me. I up with me rifle, took careful aim, and let him have it dead centre . . .'

'Hey, wait a minute!' cried Crooked Mick; 'I thought you said you had no ammo left?'

Big Barnett smashed his fist down on the bar counter, crushing a rouseabout who was fixing the beer pipes underneath it. 'Hell!' roared Barnett, 'you don't want facts. You want a ruddy argument!'

Crooked Mick was deeply offended by this remark and challenged Big Barnett to a fist fight. They adjourned to a nearby clearing on what is now called the Fifty-Mile Plain; and the greatest bare-knuckle bout of all time began. They were fairly evenly matched, for although Barnett had the weight, Mick had the speed.

Before the fight the Fifty-Mile was natural forest. When it was over there was nothing left but a dust-bowl.

The contestants raised so much dust, in fact, that at the end of the fight they couldn't tell whether it was the sun or the moon that was trying to break through the pall of darkness.

They argued about this for a long time; and even when the dust cleared they still were unable to reach any conclusion. So they asked a man who was riding by, 'Is that the sun up there, or the moon? We'll abide by your decision.'

After gazing cautiously upwards for a few moments the newcomer mumbled apologetically, 'You'll have to excuse me, gentlemen, but I can't tell. I'm a stranger round here.'

He then rode off with all possible speed.

The old-timers say that after that marathon bout of fisticuffs Big Barnett bathed himself in Sydney Harbour; and Crooked Mick washed his hands in the Yarra River.